WARNING SIGN

A DI FRANK MILLER NOVEL

JOHN CARSON

DI FRANK MILLER SERIES

Crash Point
Silent Marker
Rain Town
Watch Me Bleed
Broken Wheels
Sudden Death
Under the Knife
Trial and Error
Warning Sign
Cut Throat
Blood from a Stone
Time of Death

Frank Miller Crime Series – Books 1-3 – Box set
Frank Miller Crime Series - Books 4-6 - Box set

DCI HARRY MCNEIL SERIES
Return to Evil
Sticks and Stones
Back to Life
Dead Before You Die
Hour of Need
Blood and Tears
Devil to Pay

Where Stars Will Shine – a charity anthology compiled by Emma Mitchell, featuring a Harry McNeil short story –
The Art of War and Peace

MAX DOYLE SERIES

Final Steps
Code Red
The October Project

SCOTT MARSHALL SERIES

Old Habits

WARNING SIGN

Copyright © 2018 John Carson

Edited by Melanie Underwood
Cover by Damonza

John Carson has asserted his right under the Copyright, Designs and Patents Act 1988, to be identified as the author of this work.

This is a work of fiction. Names, characters, places, brands, media, and incidents are either the products of the author's imagination or are used fictitiously. Any resemblance to actual events, locales, or persons, living or dead, is coincidental.

Without limiting the rights under copyright reserved above, no part of this publication may be reproduced, stored in or introduced into a retrieval system, or transmitted, in any form, or by any means (electronic, mechanical, photocopying, recording, or otherwise) without the prior written permission of the author of this book. Innocence is and

All rights reserved

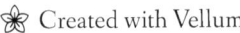 Created with Vellum

ONE

Larry Cresswell sat at the kitchen table in his vest and underpants wolfing down his second breakfast roll. His doctor had told him if he didn't start cutting out fried food, he'd die before he was sixty.

Being a contract killer, Larry thought he would die before he was fifty.

The kitchen stank of what his little friend called *a good Scottish breakfast*. It didn't matter to Larry whether it was Scottish or English, it all tasted the same. His favourite was black pudding, what the Americans called *blood pudding*. The thought made him want to recycle the fried eggs and potato scones he was washing down with lashings of tea.

He always put his breakfast on rolls. He cut the food into little bits so he could get all sorts onto the roll.

He was about to take another bite when the doorbell rang.

Larry groaned and scraped his chair back. The wee bastard had forgot his key again.

He walked along the hall and saw the outline through the door. If it was anybody taller, he wouldn't have opened it, but the small man on the other side of the frosted glass was unmistakably Scramble.

He opened the door. At six feet four, Larry was a big man, which made Scramble seem even smaller than he was.

'Jesus,' Scramble said, looking at his friend. 'Why are you answering the front door in your skids? The neighbours will think I'm a rent boy.'

'Shut up. If I was into that, I wouldn't choose a skinny wee fud like you. Besides, the house is surrounded by bushes and trees and we live in the middle of nowhere.'

'Charming. This skinny wee fud just drove into the village to get you more rolls. And a newspaper.'

Larry stood back, letting his friend and accomplice enter. 'Where's your key?'

'I forgot it, *Dad*.' He looked at Larry. 'It's Baltic outside and you're coming to the door like that. You're mental.'

'Just get in before the postie sees us.' Scramble stepped past him and Larry shut the door behind him.

'I hope you saved some scran for me,' Scramble said, walking along to the kitchen and stopping on the way to increase the temperature on the thermostat. 'It's freezing in here. You've not got the fucking window open again, have you?'

'I'm sweating like a pig,' Larry complained. 'I need my fan on.'

'Fan? For God's sake, it's December. There's snow outside.'

'Think yourself lucky that we don't sleep in the same bed.'

'In more ways than one.' Scramble put the rolls and newspaper down on the kitchen table.

'What have I told you before? Don't put the roll bag on the table. You don't know where it's been or who touched it before you. It might have germs on it.'

'It's not like the shopkeeper picked it up off the floor before putting our rolls in it.'

'Still. He might have gone for a pish and not washed his hands. You know what they're like.'

Scramble picked the bag back up and opened it, before letting the rolls slide onto a chopping board on the kitchen counter. 'That better?'

Larry made a face and grabbed a roll. 'I'm starving,' he said, going back to his chair and sitting down before his plate. He opened the paper and started reading it.

'No, children in Africa are starving. You're just...'

Larry looked at his friend to see if an insult would follow.

'A growing boy, as my mother used to say.'

Larry looked back at the paper and grabbed the half-eaten roll. 'Did you make the call?' he asked with a mouthful of food.

'Thththththth,' Scramble said, mocking him.

Larry chewed and swallowed. 'Did you make the call or not? You know, you're worse than my first wife.'

'God rest her soul,' Scramble said, putting butter on two rolls before scooping some of the Scottish breakfast from the frying pan onto a plate.

'I told you, I never killed her. She fell down the stairs.'

'For a hitman, you were taking a chance.'

'She fell down the fucking stairs. How many times do I have to tell you? Don't worry, I wouldn't throw you down the stairs. I'd just throw the toaster in the bath.' He swallowed and grinned. 'Anyway, you're one to talk; chucking that guy over the balcony. You were lucky there were no witnesses.'

'Luck has nothing to do with it. Planning, my fine friend, planning.'

Larry stabbed a fork into a piece of square sausage and held it up before shoving it into his mouth. 'What happened when you made the call?'

'We start work soon.'

'Where abouts?'

'Here. At home.'

Larry chewed for a bit then swallowed. Drank more tea. 'We're national and international, not local.'

'First of all, hopping on a jet over to Spain and spiking some old fanny's drink doesn't really count as us being international hitmen.'

'It does to me,' Larry answered, letting out a huge burp before chasing a piece of link sausage around the plate with his fork.

Scramble screwed up his face. 'Fucking charming. No wonder your second wife fucked off.' He waved a hand in front of his face.

'Bloody drama queen. Get on with it. What's the details?'

Scramble sat down at the table. 'It's tonight. I'll write it down for you. In crayon.'

Larry ignored him as he opened his copy of *The Caledonian*. 'Did you see who's coming back to town?'

'No. If it's some overpaid sports tosser, I'm not interested. Some ponce knocking a wee ball around a park, trying to get it into an old Heinz beans can they've buried in the grass. They should try working for a living. Lazy bastards.'

'No, not some ponce like that; some ponce like

this.' He picked up the paper and showed him the article.

'As I live and breathe. I never thought I'd see the day.'

'Me neither. The man was a legend. A long time ago.' He looked at Scramble. 'Get me another roll.'

TWO

'My whole life's been a lie.' Lou Purcell sat down at the dining table and poured himself a cup of tea.

'What are you talking about?' Percy Purcell said to his father. 'It's a bit early in the morning for a deep and meaningful conversation. Why don't you just look at the cartoons like you usually do?'

'What's up, Lou?' Suzy said, sitting down opposite him.

'I was going through some of my parent's papers. I was looking for an old photograph and I discovered this stuff in an envelope. Papers I hadn't seen before.'

'What sort of papers?'

Lou looked across at his daughter-in-law. 'I was adopted.'

Percy had grabbed his mug handle but didn't move

it to his mouth. 'Adopted? You never told me that before.'

'I just found out. And another year goes by without a *Detective of the Year* trophy sitting on the mantelpiece. Pay attention.'

'Why wouldn't Grandma and Grandpa tell you?'

'I don't know. But guess what my real name was?'

'Spunky McRainbow.'

'Close but no cigar. Thomas Young.'

'I can't see you as a Thomas. Spunky yes, Thomas, no.'

'It says it in black and white.'

'And you could have named me after you instead of landing me with this moniker.'

Suzy slapped Percy's wrist. 'I wouldn't have wanted to marry a Thomas. I love your name.'

'Yeah, I'm used to it now. It caused a lot of fights in school, but I won most of them. Apart from Sandy—'

'Never mind that,' Lou said, interrupting. 'Guess who my father was?'

'Jack the Ripper.'

'They never found him, remember? Apart from fighting at school, did you actually pay attention to anything?'

'They *say* they never found him.'

'That was before my father's time. No, keep guessing.'

'How would I know who your biological father was?'

'His name was Thomas Young, too.'

'Did Mum choose my name?'

'She did. I wish she had gone for my suggestion of *Richard*, so I could have shortened it. But guess what he did for a living?'

'Why did you come round here so early? I'm used to having a coffee and reading *The Caledonian* not playing parlour games.'

'Guess.'

'He was a circus midget.'

'Good God. How you've never been fired is beyond me.'

'It's not like I talk like this outside the house. I don't go shouting that around the station.'

'I should bloody well hope not. Midget indeed. They're small people. Ignoramus.'

'I'm kidding. Get on with it. There's an episode of *Fireman Sam* coming on that I don't want to miss.'

'It worries me you know a show like that and you don't have any kids.'

'Hey, I was channel-hopping one day and I noticed it. Don't judge.'

'Right, any more guesses what my father was? Suzy?'

'A police officer.'

'Nope. He was a judge!'

'You didn't give me time to guess,' Percy said. 'I was going to say that.'

'Liar.'

'I know. I was going to say he was a clown. I'm sticking with the circus theme.'

'Shut up. You're the only clown in the family. But anyway. A judge. Can you imagine? If my adopted dad had told me that, I might have chosen a different career other than banking.'

'Bank *robbing*, probably, knowing you,' Percy said.

'Ignore him, Lou,' Suzy said. 'How do you know he was a judge?'

'My mother left me a letter. It was in that envelope. I never looked in it until now because I thought it was papers that I'd seen before. She told me about it and hoped I'd forgive them for not telling me before. She wanted me to know that my mother was young and had an affair with the judge who was married and had kids. She worked in his house as a maid and they were having an affair.'

Percy drank his coffee. 'In all seriousness, I'm surprised your parents didn't tell you before they died.'

'They were proud people, Percy. I don't know if they told anybody else. They would have seen that as an embarrassment. Their son, who they adopted, was born illegitimate.'

'See? I've always said you were an old bastard.'

Despite himself, Lou laughed when he saw his son smiling. 'Just wait until you find the letter I've written, for after I pop my clogs. See where you came from.'

'That psychology doesn't work on me.'

'Ungrateful wee sod.' Lou picked up his teacup and his hand was shaking a bit. 'It's made me determined to look into this further.'

'Where are you going to start?' Suzy asked.

'One of those ancestor search sites, *Relatively Unknown* it's called. They have family trees in there and you can look at threads people have started and ask questions. They even have a DNA profile service. You spit into a plastic tube and send it to them.'

'Send yours off and they might find the missing link.'

'Always the bloody comedian. You waste your talents working as a police officer. Detective superintendent? Lollipop man more like.'

'Don't listen to him, Lou. Tell me more. This is fascinating. I used to dream that I was really a princess and I had been given away when I was a baby and one day, the king came looking for me.'

Percy rolled his eyes. 'When they put the straitjacket on him, they'll want to know what set him off, and I'll point them in your direction.'

'Anyway, if I can join some thread, maybe a

family member out there will get in touch. And if I do the DNA thing, then they match you up with other people throughout the world that you're related to.'

'Prince Philip's quaking in his boots right now, I'm sure.'

Lou ignored his son. 'I'm going to look anyway. I want to see if there are other members of my family I don't know about.'

'How old do you think this judge is? You're in your early sixties, so he must be a fair age, if he's even alive.'

'I know that. But I seem to have half siblings. I'd like to reach out to them.'

'Are you sure that's a good idea? I mean, how would you approach them? *Hello there. You don't know me, but your old man got my mother up the duff and now I want to meet up.* They might tell you to go raffle yourself.'

'The answer's always no unless you ask. If I write to them and ask them to meet up, then it's a bonus if they say yes.'

'They might think you're after the family coffers.'

'Not everybody is suspicious like you.'

'It's my job to be suspicious of people.'

'Some people might think it's great having a family member they didn't know existed.'

'If you were a billionaire. Some people might get

upset that their father was entertaining a member of staff.'

'Just tread with caution,' Suzy said.

'What does Elizabeth think of all this?' Percy said.

'I don't know. I haven't asked her.'

'You haven't seen her this morning?'

'It's Friday.'

'What's that got to do with the price of cheese?'

'We meet for lunch on a Friday. Besides, I don't know if I want to tell every Tom, Dick, and Harry.'

'She's your girlfriend. That's something that a boyfriend should tell his girlfriend. I mean, what if she wants to have your children?'

'Manky wee sod. I respect Elizabeth.'

'No you don't. You asked her to move in with you and she knocked you back.'

'That was her daft laddie putting a spanner in the works. He's even dafter than you.'

'She's a lady, you said. But that didn't stop you asking her to live in sin with you.'

'*You* did it.' Lou looked at Suzy. 'No offence, Suzy.'

'None taken.'

'It was different for me and Suzy,' Percy said. 'You're too old for those shenanigans.'

'*Too old*? Speak for yourself.'

'She would have moved in with you if you'd married her.'

'I wasn't going to marry her. First of all, as I just said, her laddie's lift doesn't go all the way to the top floor. And if I'd married her, she would have got her claws into me.'

'I know what you mean.'

'Percy!' Suzy said.

'Present company excepted. I mean some women are just out for what they can get.'

'Well, I'm a lot smarter than that,' Lou said.

'It's true though. You would have married her and Quasi Modo would have been sniffing round, looking to sleep on your couch.'

'Aye, sod that for a laugh. He came round the other week and he was bogging. Clarty sod could think of taking a shower now and again.'

'So, you're not going to tell her?' Suzy said.

'No. In fact, I was going to tell you this eventually, but we decided to go our own way.'

'I'm not surprised,' Percy said.

'Don't get me wrong, I liked her a lot, but she has *two* sons, one of them is normal and the other one looks like he should have run away to the circus.'

'Clarty the Clown.'

'Exactly.'

'Are you upset about it, Lou?' Suzy asked.

'Naw. I feel relieved, to be honest. I'm thinking about renting my flat out and moving back in here.'

'Lou, as much as I lov... lov... like you, I don't think it would be a wise idea. Don't get me wrong...' Percy said.

'Look at him. Trying to think on his feet. I'm your father, not the Marquis De Sade. Relax. I'm kidding. Now that I'm settled into my wee flat and Elizabeth is gone, I can do my own thing again. Elizabeth was tying me down. I want to spend my time looking for my family.'

'If you need our help, just call us,' Suzy said.

'I will.'

'I've just had a thought,' Percy said.

'Oh, here we go. Mark it on the calendar. He had a thought.'

'No, seriously. I want to ask you; was I adopted?'

Lou laughed. 'I wish. I would have given you back.'

'That was a serious question. I mean, it would explain a lot.'

'Like?'

'Like how I'm good-looking, witty, intelligent.'

'When they were handing out wits, you apparently only got half.'

'If I was adopted, I would sue the agency. Sticking me with you.'

'Sorry to disappoint you, son, but I was there when you came sliding right out of your mother's birth canal.'

'Jesus Christ. Have a word with yourself. There's

just some things you can't unimagine.' Percy stood up from the table as Lou sat grinning. 'He makes Steptoe look like a choirboy.'

'You're too young to remember that show.'

'I've seen it on YouTube. But... some of us have to work.'

'I'll let you know how my search works out. Introduce you to some new cousins if I find any.'

'Don't bother. It just means more Christmas presents to buy. And if they're all as daft as you, I'll pass, thanks.'

THREE

'Frank? Do babies eat pizza?'

'No, honey. They just drink milk for a while.'

'Oh, okay,' Emma said, eating her cereal on the couch, watching *Fireman Sam*. 'So, tonight, we'll have pizza but Annie won't be having any.'

'That's right. When she gets older, she'll have plenty of pizza.'

'I love my baby sister, Frank.'

'Me too. I love you both.' He leaned down and kissed his stepdaughter on the cheek. Then he walked through to the kitchen where he put on the coffee. Outside, it was snowing again. His wife, Kim, was putting the baby down again after feeding her. It still felt unreal that it was only a week since the new addition to their family finally arrived.

Little Annie Miller, seven pounds, five ounces. Of course, he loved his stepdaughter, Emma, but just to see the little life that he had helped create made him fall in love with her.

It was just a few short months ago that a bullet had narrowly missed him and Kim at their wedding, a gunman intent on finishing what somebody else had started. It was somebody who had never been on Miller's radar; the man who had bought the hotel in Stockbridge, where Miles Laing used to work. He had been working for the people who had wanted Miller dead.

'A week until Christmas and I haven't even got half the shopping done,' Kim said, coming into the kitchen. She was slowly losing her baby weight but the bump wasn't going down quickly enough for her.

'You have a baby to look after now, Mrs Miller, so don't go getting stressed out. Samantha said she would help out. Jack too. We have a lot of help at hand.'

'I know. I just wanted to get you something special for Christmas.'

'You've already given me something special, remember? She's through there sleeping. And the other one is watching cartoons.'

She smiled at him, pulling her nightgown tighter around herself. 'I want to join a gym as soon as I can.'

'It's not like you need to join a gym.'

'Miller, you are such a good liar, but I'm your wife, I can see right through your lies. Thanks, anyway.' She took the coffee and sipped at the black liquid. 'What have you got going on today?'

'Well, I thought I would fly down to Spain to see if my captain has the boat ready, then I might sail round the Med for a little bit. Do some sea fishing.'

'First of all, you don't fish. And without me? Forget about it.'

'Oh, alright, I'll stay here and do some detective work.' He drank some of his own coffee, his back to the window. 'I have to liaise with a man called Adrian Jackson. He's coming back to Edinburgh.'

'What's so special about Mr Jackson?'

'I don't know him personally, but Jack knew him, years ago. He was half Scottish, half American. He lived over here, in Edinburgh. He was a businessman, owned a few clubs. Then he went for a stay in America for a while. His father was dying, so he wanted to spend time with him. The story goes, he was playing a game of poker, some trouble started, and one of the men got shot. By Jackson. He said the gun went off by accident but they didn't believe him, and he got charged with second degree murder. He served fifteen years. Then a witness came forward after all this time and confirmed Jackson's story. His sentence was commuted to second degree manslaughter, and they released him.'

'Why is he coming back here?'

'I'll ask him when I see him. Me and Percy Purcell are driving out to the airport to pick him up. Our new justice minister said he has to be met at the airport for his own safety.'

'His safety?'

Miller walked over to the sink and rinsed his mug out before putting it on the drainer.

'That's just a ruse. He wants me and Percy to give him a warning. He was either always getting into trouble, or trouble followed him around. We're going to give him the usual story about how we'll be watching him.'

'I wish I was going.'

'I'm sure your mother will give you the rundown on him. Norma will want to meet him as part of the Procurator Fiscal contingent.'

'Jackson sounds like a nice man. Not.'

'I can't wait to see what all the fuss is about. And not only him, we're meeting his wife too. Fiona Jackson. I've heard of her, I just didn't know she was his wife.'

'Is she American?'

'No. She runs a few pubs of his here.'

'I'm sure this Jackson guy will be an easy job for you.'

'Let's hope so.'

'How old is he?'

'Early fifties. Fifty-three, fifty-four, I think.'

'Some old bloke comes back to Scotland and needs his hand held. How hard can it be?'

FOUR

'Some old bloke in his fifties?' Percy Purcell said as he pulled into the car park of the Edinburgh Airport Police Office, at Almond Avenue, on the periphery of the terminal.

'She doesn't know Jackson at all. Neither do I. Just what I was given to read up on him.'

'He's a bad bastard, and no mistake,' Purcell said. 'I had dealings with him plenty of times. When I heard he'd been arrested in America and the key thrown away, I sighed with relief. I was shocked when I heard one of those dozy American prosecutors had now struck a deal with him. I wonder how that came about?'

'I was talking to Samantha about the case, since she's from over there, and a lot of it is political. A prosecutor running for judge needs the votes. Yes, Jackson was a victory for a prosecutor, but not the one who's in power now. By doing this deal, the move was reported on and suddenly this prosecutor has his name in the papers,' said Miller.

'And as if by magic, a new witness turns up and says he was there at the time. Very convenient.'

'Apparently, he could prove it.'

'I think they just wanted rid of him. Jackson always maintained his innocence, and his wife was always stirring up trouble, so the prosecutor gets a double whammy; his name in the paper and the loud mouth out of the country,' said Purcell.

'The prosecutor's now a judge. They get voted in. They don't care how they win a case, as long as they win.'

Two officers who were waiting to do their stint on patrol inside the airport were waiting for them in the Land Rover just at the station entrance.

Snow was blowing gently, and it hadn't been enough to cancel the United flight from Newark in New Jersey.

'Do you think being a cop at the airport is an easy number?' Purcell asked Miller before they got out of the car.

'Dealing with irate airline passengers? No, I don't.'

'But you get to carry a machine gun.'

'That would sway my decision if I was applying.

Sometimes I wish *we* carried machine guns. Christ, we don't even get to carry pistols.'

'Now, now, Frank. You know there are no guns in the UK and we don't need to arm ourselves.' Purcell made a face as he opened the passenger door and got out into an icy wind.

They walked over to the Land Rover and climbed into the back.

'Morning, lads,' Purcell said.

'Morning, sir,' the passenger said. He was a sergeant and the team leader for this patrol.

'They've told you why we're here?'

'They have indeed. And rather you than me.'

'Why's that?'

'My old man was a copper too. He was smacked by Jackson one night. I might be tempted to give Jackson a little taste of his own medicine.'

'I'm sure there's a queue. That's why we're here to bring him and his other half back to the city centre.'

The Land Rover pulled out and drove for thirty seconds to a parking area just off the bus lane. They all got out and walked through the entrance to the international arrivals' hall.

A woman walked forward when she saw the two uniforms come in, and Purcell stepped forward. 'Detective Superintendent Purcell, DI Miller. We're here for Adrian Jackson.'

'If you'll follow me, sir.'

Upstairs in the management corridor, they were taken along to a conference room. The woman knocked and entered, followed by the two detectives.

Inside was a man in a suit sitting at a rectangular table, with another man in a suit and a woman sitting at the opposite end.

Adrian Jackson stood up. For a man in his fifties, he looked fit. He was dressed in an expensive-looking blazer with a polo shirt. An overcoat was draped over the back of the leather chair he'd been sitting in. A bowler hat sat on the table in front of him.

The woman who sat beside him wore a fur coat, but whether it was fake or real, Miller couldn't tell.

'As I live and breathe, if it isn't young Percy Purcell!' Jackson said, almost shouting. 'They didn't tell me the best detective in Lothian and Borders was coming to pick me up!'

'He couldn't make it, so they sent me instead.'

'Nonsense! You're too modest, young Percy!' Jackson grabbed hold of the walking stick that Miller hadn't noticed and walked round the table to greet Purcell. He walked up and hugged him like he would an old friend.

Purcell gently pushed him away.

'And who do we have here?' Jackson looked at Miller, his smile still firmly in place.

'This is DI Frank Miller. He'll be liaising with you for a while. Just to make sure your transition is smooth.'

Miller quickly stuck out his hand before Jackson could move in for a hug, and Jackson shook it, his grip firm, no doubt from working out in his prison cell in an effort to keep his privates intact.

'They didn't tell me you walked with a stick, Jackson,' Purcell said.

'Since when did we use last names?' He sat back down. 'I was attacked in my cell by two thugs. They did something to my spine, some medical name. I need to rely on it when I'm going to be on my feet for a while.'

'I hope the two thugs involved got the full weight of the justice system brought down on them,' Miller said.

Jackson laughed, and said with a hint of sarcasm in his voice, 'Let's just say, their boss was dealt with and I never had trouble again.'

'Adrian, watch what you're saying,' said Richard Sullivan, the man in the suit and Jackson's lawyer.

'You've been keeping a low profile lately, haven't you, Richard?' Miller said.

'Keeping busy, Inspector Miller.' Sullivan and Miller had history. To say there was animosity between them was perhaps an exaggeration, but there was always going to be a certain distrust between them. They co-existed with a mutual respect, but whenever there was a high-profile case from which money was to be made, Sullivan was always there.

'You know my lovely wife, Fiona?' Jackson said, eager to get the attention back to himself.

'Indeed I do,' Purcell said, 'but only from what I've been briefed on.'

Fiona Jackson was a couple of years younger than her husband but had been spending his money on keeping herself looking youthful. If Miller didn't know better, he would say she was ten years younger.

'I'm hoping that after you've given us the *Stay safe and behave yourself* lecture, we can go back to enjoying our life together,' Fiona said.

'That's our aim,' Purcell said, sitting down and indicating for Miller to do the same. 'While you were away at the New York Butlins, we had some problems with a certain group after they bought your clubs and businesses.'

Jackson put on a mock concerned look. 'Yes, Fiona did tell me that some desperate interlopers stepped in to buy my properties, but we managed to keep ourselves afloat.'

'If there's any trouble, we want you to call us and let us deal with it,' Miller said.

'Of course,' Jackson said. 'You and Percy boy will be the first people I call if I get a rogue Pakistani calling me and telling me I owe money to the Inland Revenue.

I find it strange how all these government departments have to close because of lack of money, but they spend a fortune on changing everything, like their stationery. Don't you?'

'I want you to take this seriously,' Purcell said.

'I am. I'm just joshing with you, Percy my old son. I'm home to start off on a new foot. Clean slate. I just want to get back to my life of being an honest businessman.'

Sullivan spoke up. 'I know you have to give him this talk, detective, but rest assured I have already been in discussion with my client. He doesn't want any unsolicited media attention.'

'Except on Facebook, where it was announced to the world he was coming back home,' Miller said.

Jackson laughed again. 'Fiona is my media manager. It was her idea to put my release on Facebook. After all, it's already been reported in the papers, so it's not like we announced to the world that we found the Holy Grail.'

'I think a lot more people look at Facebook than read the papers.' Miller locked eyes with the man for a moment, knowing exactly why his wife had put the release on Facebook; she was announcing to the world that Adrian was back, and bring it on if you think you're hard enough.

'That's as may be, but I'm not going to hide from anybody.'

'Having said that, we have a security team in place,' Fiona said.

Jackson stopped smiling and bobbed his head up and down a few times. 'This is merely to dissuade the unfortunate souls who do not have a grasp of right and wrong to stop coming up to me. It's why celebrities have bodyguards. I for one don't want a little piece of Princes Street gardens created into my version of Strawberry Fields.'

'A celebrity now, are we?' Purcell said.

'Of sorts. Just because I haven't been on a celebrity jungle show doesn't mean some people wouldn't want to have a pop.'

'I don't think you'll have to worry about anybody digging up Princes Street Gardens for you,' Miller said. 'Maybe they would donate a bench with your name on a plaque or something.'

'I can see that being a police officer has jaded you a little bit,' Jackson said to Miller. 'And this being the time of year when there's goodwill to all men. But whatever you've heard about me, all I can say is, the stories are greatly exaggerated. You know what Chinese whispers are like; I start off by being a businessman in Edinburgh and end up being a brutal gangster. But I want to believe that you will all do the right thing, should I find myself in need of your help.'

'You'll get any help you need, just like any other member of the public,' Purcell said.

'Where are you going to be staying?' Miller asked.

'Why, where else would I stay? But in my new apartment in Ravelston.'

'What happened to your house in Murrayfield?'

'It was sold to fund my campaign for justice.'

'And now you're living in a flat,' Purcell said.

'It's not a manky wee tenement, Percy. Besides, it's better than the six by ten I lived in before. And this is just a stop gap until I win my lawsuit for false imprisonment in the States.'

Sullivan looked at Purcell. 'Will that be all?'

Purcell looked at Miller before looking over to Jackson. 'I think we're done here. But I would appreciate a weekly meeting, so we can go over any security concerns. Meantime, DI Miller and a member of his team will be calling round to see that you're safe.'

'Coming round for a wee neb at the new digs, more like.' He winked at Miller. 'Call my wife.'

The two detectives stood up. 'Where would you like us to drop you off?'

'Nowhere. I'm taking the new tram to Haymarket, then we can get a taxi to take us from there.'

'You might be safer taking a taxi directly from here,' Miller said.

'I'm glad you take my safety to heart, Inspector Miller, but I assure you, there's no need. I'm looking forward to walking about in the bracing Scottish air. New York was fine, but the temperatures are a bit extreme. At least here in Edinburgh, it's more or less the same season all year round, with only a slight variation. Sorry you had a wasted trip.'

'It wasn't wasted. I got to meet you and your wife.'

'Putting a face to the legend, eh, Miller? I hope you're not disappointed.'

'We'll be checking in with you, Jackson.'

'Just let him know in advance that you're coming for a visit,' Sullivan said.

'Yeah, that's what we'll do.'

'You know you're going to be mobbed by reporters when you get on that tram?' Miller said.

'Of course he does,' Purcell said. 'That's why Sullivan is here. Nothing like a little free promo when you're writing a book, is there, Dickie?'

'Even bad publicity is free publicity,' Sullivan answered with a barely disguised grin.

FIVE

Snow was falling lightly as Michael Molloy paced back and forth in his new office overlooking Waverley Station. His father, Robert, walked in and took off his overcoat.

'I'm not sure I like the idea of being so close to Frank Miller's gaff,' Michael said.

'Fuck's sake. On the peeve already?' Robert said, hanging up his coat and walking over to the drinks' cabinet. 'I need a little snifter to warm my cockles.'

Robert took a fine crystal decanter out and poured himself a healthy measure. He held up the glass vessel and his son nodded. Robert topped him up.

'Might as well. You're only here once after all. And God knows that fucking head contractor is doing my tits in.' Michael took a swig of the whisky.

Robert poured another measure, this one for

himself and put the decanter away. They clinked their fine glasses and sat down on leather chairs near a window.

'I'm thinking of having a wee holiday after Christmas,' Robert said. 'Somewhere warm. No snow, just sunshine.'

'Lucky you,' said Michael. 'I have to stay here and whip these morons into shape.'

'It will be worth it in the end, you'll see.'

Robert Molloy had bought the old Scotsman hotel on the North Bridge and was currently turning it into an even swankier hotel. It wouldn't be able to compete with the Balmoral sitting opposite but it would come close.

'I suppose. But let me tell you, if I hear about any more problems with the lavvies downstairs, I swear I'm going to shove that fucking foreman's head down one.'

'Relax, Michael. It's still a few days until the official opening and everything will be running like a Swiss watch by then.'

'Unlike now. It's running like a fucking piece of Swiss cheese.'

'You'll give yourself a coronary. And you wouldn't want that now, would you? You're not going to do Izzy any good when you're lying in a box.'

Michael grinned and drank some whisky. 'You're right there. I can't wait to show her the place here.'

'That's why I'm here. The contractor and I had a sit down yesterday and I advised him that his health too might take a turn for the worse if all the permits weren't ready by end of closing today. We have that crime festival thing going on here and we've already accepted bookings for Christmas and I will not be made to look like a twat. I also promised him a healthy bonus, off the books.'

'Money talks. Mind you, so would a reciprocating saw and a darkened room in the basement of the club.'

'You catch more flies with honey than vinegar.'

'Didn't stop you in the past.'

'That was business. You don't have to be nice on the way up when you have no intention of coming back down.' He smiled and raised his own glass. 'I'm hungry. I have been assured that the kitchens are up and running and all the staff are familiarising themselves with the food and tools. Let's get them to make us breakfast.'

'I'm trying to watch my weight. I should maybe just have oats.'

'Time for your oats when you get home tonight, Michael. Get a bacon roll down your throat.'

'Aye, fuck it. Make it two. If I'm hungry, I'll be bad tempered and that will lead to somebody going through the station roof after I throw them out the window.'

'Then there really would be a Flying Scotsman in the Waverley.'

They left the office and ventured downstairs to one of the restaurants. The hotel was basically finished with just the spit and polish needed to make her shine.

The contractor was bustling about the reception area. Robert Molloy had told him that he didn't want to see a pair of jeans in the hotel.

The maître d' was busy with staff but rushed over when he saw Molloy. 'Good morning, sir. Are you dining?'

'My son and I would like to sample some breakfast, Henri,' Robert said. 'And get me a copy of today's *Caledonian.*'

'As opposed to yesterday's?' Michael said.

They were shown to a table overlooking the Waverley. The same view as they had from their office, only lower down.

'Don't be a smartarse, especially in front of the staff,' Robert said to his son.

'I'm only joking.'

'Don't.'

Henri brought a copy of the paper and took their orders. After he bustled away, Robert spread out the paper on the table.

'Fuck me.'

'What is it now? Your shares in quail eggs gone down?'

'Again with the smartarse.' Robert shook his head and looked out at the snow-covered glass roof of the train station, like his mind was taking him somewhere else. 'Guess who's back in town?'

'Well, I know Santa isn't due for another week, so let me see... nope, I don't know.'

'Jackson.'

'Michael?'

Robert looked at his son with raised eyebrows and shook his head slightly. 'Adrian.'

'Adrian Jackson? Oh, yeah, Dad, I read about that a while ago. They were getting him back into court to do some deal. I knew he was getting out sometime.'

'I haven't seen his wife, Fiona, for a while.'

'She's been keeping a low profile.'

A waitress came across with a carafe of orange juice and poured both men a glass.

'Thanks, love,' Michael said.

'Why don't we ask him when we see him?' Robert said.

'You're not serious?'

'I am. I want to have a word in his ear.' Robert sipped some orange juice as the girl brought a coffee pot over and then the bacon rolls were delivered. When the staff were gone, he took a bite of his roll and wiped his face with a napkin. 'Jesus, these rolls are the business.'

'Bloody good,' Michael agreed. 'But carry on about Jackson.'

'Well, you do know he used to own our place in George Street?'

'The Club?'

'Yes.' Molloy had recently bought a restaurant in George Street, and he owned several pubs and clubs around the city.

'When was this?'

'Before you'd ever had your first fag.'

'I had my first fag when I was thirteen, Dad.'

'Did you now, you wee bugger? Anyway, the club was his before he was picked up in America. A lot of his assets were sold off and that place was one of them. I snapped it up at a great price.' Robert drank some coffee. 'That was twenty-five years ago.'

'And you think he'll want to buy it back.'

'He can fuck off if he does.'

The maître d' came back over. 'Is everything alright, Mr Molloy?'

'Yes, Henri. Nothing to do with this place.'

'Very good, sir.'

'You don't think this Jackson twat will come here to see you, do you, Dad?'

'I'll have some of the boys take him for a joyride if he does.'

'Surely, he'd have to be deranged to come here?'

'I'll put some feelers out, but Jackson still has a lot of connections in the city. Technically, he still owns some boozers.'

'Which ones?' said Michael.

'Just some shitey places that probably had sawdust on the floor not that long ago.'

'Where does he stay?'

'He used to live in Murrayfield. God knows where he'll be staying now. But he did have quite a bit of real estate in the city, so he will have somewhere to stay.' Robert ate more of his roll. 'Get some of the boys to dig deep into his background. To be honest, I'd never thought about him after he was put away. But now I want to know everything there is to know about him.'

'I'll get onto it this morning. But I'm assuming he's dangerous?'

'He was a hard man back in the day, Michael. Not hard enough to bother me, of course. His old man was a tit, but young Jackson was the one with the screw loose. He ran with some likeminded individuals, and they got into trouble, but Jackson was the one who stood out and got himself a reputation.'

'I can't wait to meet the wee bastard,' Michael said.

'If he wants to see his old club, I'll get the boys to give him a tour of the vaults.'

'Just be on your guard. I have no doubt he'll be in touch. And if I know him, he'll want back what he sees as rightfully his.'

'I'll give him what's coming to him alright.' Michael ate some more and drank the coffee. 'How did he end up in prison over there?'

'The details are sketchy for me, but I know one thing for sure; if he messes with us, it won't be prison he'll have to worry about.'

SIX

'She wants to go to university in Glasgow,' Jeni Bridge said to her ex-husband. 'That should suit you.' She sat at the breakfast bar in the kitchen.

Alistair Bridge was usually more imposing when he had his chief constable's uniform on, but today he was just another man wearing jeans and a shirt. His heavy overcoat hung on the back of one of the stools.

'Look, it's her life,' he replied, sipping some of his own coffee. He held up a hand when he saw she was about to speak. 'I know it's going to be more convenient for me, but it's not like we fight over the custody.'

Jeni smoked her cigarette like prohibition on them was about to kick in. 'I'm going to miss her.'

'First of all, it's not going to be until next autumn. And secondly, it's a forty-five-minute drive. It's not like she's going to the University of Sydney. If there's such a thing.'

She looked out of the kitchen window at the Pentland Hills in the far distance, looking as though they'd had flour sprinkled on them. The house was a relatively new build on Craigs Road, part of Corstorphine on the west side of the city.

'When I look at her, all I see is the little girl I used to push in her pram to the library.'

'She's practically a woman now, love.' He reached over and squeezed her hand.

'That's why you're the chief constable and I'm not. You always know when to say the right things.'

'It's no cushy number, believe me. And you will get there one day, Jeni. It's there for the taking.'

'Being Commander of the Edinburgh Division of Police Scotland is hard enough. It's the bunch of detectives I work with that keep me on the straight and narrow.'

'Are you sure you don't want to come through to Glasgow for a wee hooly?'

'Alistair, as much as I appreciate your offer, your significant other doesn't want another woman in her kitchen, especially one you used to sleep with.'

'She's fine. She wouldn't mind.'

Jeni took in a deep breath and stared at the Pentlands, her mind rummaging about in her memory bank, to pick out images of her little girl when she was just a toddler.

A tear rolled down her cheek and she quickly wiped it away. Then she took another drag and blew it out into a room already filled with the poisonous fumes.

'It's going to be okay, Jeni.' Alistair's hand was rubbing her back now, up by her shoulder, and if she didn't know any better, she would think he was trying it on with her.

They heard the bedroom door close upstairs and the sound of their daughter coming down. Her little girl, now on the threshold of becoming a woman. Jeni wanted to hurt somebody.

'Right, Mum, that's me ready. I'll call you on Christmas.'

'You'll call me every day, young lady.' She stubbed out the cigarette in the ashtray in front of her.

'Okay, every day, Mum,' she said in the voice of a demented troll.

'I mean it. Don't upset Mummy now, or she'll have to put you in handcuffs and keep you in your room,' she said, half-jokingly.

'I'll call you,' her daughter said, putting the little suitcase down and giving her mother a hug. 'And as a special bonus, I'll Facetime you on Christmas morning.'

'Don't play with me.'

'No, I will, honestly.'

They pulled apart. 'You'd better, young lady. That man there might be your father and the chief big wig, but I'm a woman and I could do things to hurt him that he hasn't even dreamt of yet.'

'God, you're giving me the shivers, Jeni,' Alistair said, pulling his overcoat on.

'I remember when I used to give you a different kind of shiver.' She smiled at him.

'Aw, come on now, Mum. I haven't had breakfast yet.' Her daughter screwed up her face.

'You got your Christmas pressie?' Jeni asked her.

'Yes. And I have clean underwear, and my phone charger.'

'Good.' Jeni didn't tell her daughter that she had added a tracking plan to her phone account so she could see where her daughter was at all times. She would have called it spying software if she'd found out and Jeni didn't want any arguments before her daughter went through to Glasgow.

'Right, you ready to see Dad's new Range Rover?'

'Oh yes. I'll bet it can handle the snow better than mum's Golf.'

'Hey, that Golf has served you well as a taxi when you were drunk and wanted a lift home.'

Alistair looked at his daughter. 'Underage drinking?'

'No. Mum's taxi, yes, drinking, no. She's exaggerating.'

'Good.' Alistair picked up his daughter's case and Jeni mouthed *sorry* as her daughter made a face.

'We pinkie swore, remember?' she said, hugging her mother again.

'Sorry, it slipped out,' Jeni said, but she wondered if it had been a subconscious attempt to sabotage her daughter's stay with her father.

'Come on, honey. Dad took the day off so he could spend it with you,' Alistair said from the hallway.

'Stay safe. Call me when you get there. And let me know...'

The front door closed behind her daughter. She had taken a day off too, but now she had nothing to do with herself for the rest of the day. Go down to the Gyle Centre maybe? Get a bus into town and get pished? Number two idea far outweighed number one idea. But drinking on her own? One of her friends was a hairdresser and she only worked part-time and that was going to a customers' houses. Maybe she was off, and they could both go into town and get blootered.

Then her phone rang.

'It's DCI Gibb, ma'am.'

'You know I'm not on duty today, don't you, Paddy?'

'Yes, and I'm sorry about calling you at home, but I thought you'd want to know about this one.'

'What's happened?'

'We got a shout out to a house in The Grange. Life extinct. The doctor's just confirmed. Our subject was stabbed in the ear with a pen.'

'You can handle that, can't you?'

'Yes, we can, but I thought you'd want to know as he was sitting at a desk in his home office. And he had written your name in a notebook.'

SEVEN

'Got your cheapies for the day?' Fiona Jackson said, closing the taxi door behind her. One of the photographers who had followed them onto the tram from the airport was poking his camera into the fast black as it pulled away from the station.

'How many people are going to die, now you're back in town, Jackson?' somebody from the crowd shouted.

Jackson made a face like he was trying to pass a kidney stone then shut the window.

'There are always going to be people who think you should never have been let out,' Fiona said, putting a hand on his arm.

'Fuck 'em. I have my supporters. The rest can bog off.' He looked at the taxi driver looking at him in the rear-view mirror. 'Where are you on the spectrum, son? Adrian Jackson, guilty or innocent?'

'If you say you're innocent, Mr Jackson, then that's good enough for me,' the driver said in his best, *please give me a big tip* voice.

'Good man.' He turned to Fiona. 'Make sure you look after him when he drops us off.'

It was only a ten-minute drive to the Jackson abode in the upmarket area of Ravelston, a hop, skip, and jump from Murrayfield and the famous rugby stadium.

'I'm going to have to get a team together again. Most of the others jumped ship when I got sent down.'

'I have some in mind. Young guys who don't mind getting their hands dirty.'

'I don't care how intelligent they are, as long as they're loyal and have hands like shovels.' Jackson turned towards his wife. 'And to answer your question, no, I haven't had enough cheapies for the day.'

He looked out of the window as the cab sped towards Roseburn, and past the Roseburn bar, where he'd once broken a man's nose.

'It still feels strange,' he said.

'What does?' Fiona said.

He looked into her eyes. 'That I'm back home with my wife. You could have dumped me and had your pick of men.'

'I know this might sound corny, but I fell in love

with you the moment I first saw you. Nobody could come close. I knew one day you would come back to me. I knew you were innocent.'

'That's amazing. I don't think even my lawyer thought I was innocent.'

'Women's intuition.'

The taxi pulled into the car park of the luxury apartment complex.

'You've done well, getting us this place,' he said to her as the cab stopped at the main entrance and Fiona paid the fare.

'When you gave me power of attorney, I cut the dead wood,' she said as they got out and went into the main lobby. 'I sold the properties that were going to drag us down and invested some money in this place.'

'Very nice. I'm impressed so far.'

'It used to belong to a surgeon.'

'I hope he didn't fucking die in bed.'

They rode the lift up to one of the penthouse flats.

'Not as far as I'm aware.'

Inside, the flat had been decorated with the best of furniture. Jackson felt something in his gut; repulsion. Maybe it was from spending so much time in an eight by ten, but this place looked like something out of an upper-crust magazine, specially laid out for a photographer. It wasn't to his taste at all.

'It's beautiful,' he said, turning to his wife. He

hugged her in case she could see the lie in his eyes. He thought it was the most hideous junk he had ever clapped eyes on. Antique furniture, a leather couch with wooden arms. What the fuck was she thinking? He pulled apart from her.

'Now get rid of it.'

'What?' She looked puzzled.

'You heard. This is utter shite. I don't like any of it.'

'You just said it was beautiful.'

'I didn't want to upset you, but if we're going to get off on the right foot, I have to be honest with you. It's hideous. I appreciate you going to this trouble but get rid of it.'

She smiled. 'I wasn't sure what you would like after getting out, so I had a staging company in to throw pieces of furniture around until we could go shopping together. It's here for a week. We can order our own stuff and then the staging company can come and get it.'

He smiled at her. 'You're a very smart girl.' He took in a deep breath and let it out slowly. 'Get them to pick it up tomorrow.'

'I have a woman come in and clean and look after the place. An older woman. I trust her, but I had her background gone over. She's clean. If you'll pardon the pun. And I have a surprise for you.' She walked over to the couch where a shiny black cane was leaning against it. 'I had it specially made.'

He took it and she showed him the special feature it had.

'Good girl.' He paused for a moment. 'I know we haven't, you know...' He nodded towards her, hoping he wouldn't have to spell it out.

'We can go through now, if you like?'

'I do like, but the problem is, I haven't done this in a long time, and I'm not only out of practise but bloody knackered.'

'Don't worry, my love, we have the rest of our lives together.'

'Show me where the bedroom is anyway. I want to put my stuff away.'

She showed him where it was and then went back and picked up the pile of mail on the side table in the living room.

'There's a letter for you,' she said when he came back in.

He opened it and looked at it before showing it to his wife. In blood-red letters, written on the paper, were the words – GO HOME JACKSON. OR YOU WILL DIE.

'Oh my God,' Fiona said, putting a hand to her mouth.

'There are some people who don't want to see me

back in Edinburgh,' her husband replied. 'People who would obviously rather see me dead.' He turned to her. 'I won't be run out of town.'

Fiona's breath was coming fast. 'I'm scared, Adrian.'

'You don't have to be. I'll be looking after you.' *And when I find out who did this, the red won't be ink on paper.*

EIGHT

The Golf made it just fine up to The Grange. Jeni Bridge parked behind the posse of emergency vehicles.

The house was large, in its own grounds. Some monster a long time ago had thought it a good idea to divide the house into flats. Now three people called this home, instead of one. It was a traditional sandstone detached, with a single garage on the left. Jeni wondered who got use of it.

She pulled up the collar of her overcoat, her boots crunching on the fallen snow.

Techs were coming in and out of the house. A woman wearing jeans and a cardigan was standing just inside the hallway, holding a hanky to her nose and mouth, like she couldn't decide whether to cough or blow.

'Who's that?' she asked Paddy Gibb.

'One of the tenants. There's three owners, but the flat on your right belongs to a guy who is currently in Thailand chasing wee lassies.'

'Very sceptical, Paddy. Talking from experience?'

'God, no. Isn't that what all single young men do in Thailand?'

'I don't know. I haven't been and I'm not a single young man.' She looked at him with a grin that was half grimace. 'You've just reminded me I'm single and now I feel sad that I'm going to be alone on Christmas day. Good job, Paddy. You should be a social worker.'

'Oh, sorry, I just meant-'

'Relax. I don't mind. My daughter is spending the holiday with her father, which will be a barrel of laughs. And being the chief constable, I doubt very much, he'll be dressing up as Santa Claus. Just one photo on social media and your career's down the lavvy.'

'You know all about that, don't you, Paddy?' DS Andy Gibb said, coming along the hallway from the doorway on the right. Jeni could feel the cold from outside having a fight with the heat from inside.

'You're the one who messes about putting photos up on that Instant Gram thing.'

'Instagram.' *Grandpa* he mouthed behind Jeni's back as she stepped out of the way of a tech.

'Maybe you could show the commander inside,' Gibb said, sticking two fingers up at Watt.

'This way,' Watt said, leading the way.

'If this young man is away in foreign climes, who lives here?'

'It's one of those rental properties, listed on a rental website. Where people rent your house for a holiday.'

'I've heard of that. *Come and fuck my house while I'm in Benidorm.* Something like that.'

'I don't know why anybody would want to rent it to a bunch of yahoos who get pished and trash the place. This place is rented through a site called, *Home from Home.* According to the agency who deals with the bookings, the victim was booked here for almost two weeks.'

There was a door on the right, which would have led into a drawing room, many moons ago before a developer got his hands on it.

It was a TV room and office combined. The victim was sitting at the desk, slumped over. They could see blood coming out of his right ear where the pen was still sticking out.

'The pen is indeed mightier than the sword,' Jeni said, walking closer. Then to Gibb, 'You said he had written my name?'

'It's in the open notebook by his left hand.'

His right hand was hanging down by his right side,

while the left was indeed on the book. She stepped closer, careful not to touch anything and looked over his shoulder. And there it was, in black and white. *Jeni Bridge*. Right above *Amber Summers*.

She turned to the doctor who had come back into the room. Pathologist, Jake Dagger.

'Can I move him?' she asked.

'Sure. I can have some of my staff get him off the chair.'

'No, I just want to see his face.'

Dagger walked over, still dressed in his forensic suit and waved Gibb over. Gibb nodded to Watt. 'My back's hurting just now. Get over there, son.'

'How did you hurt your back?' Watt asked grinning. He looked over at the head of forensics, DI Maggie Parks. Watt knew she and Gibb had been going out together for a few months.

'Just get a bloody move on.' He reached into his pocket for his cigarettes and brought the packet out. *Go on, we dare you to light one of us up in front of your boss. Go on, you horrible old bastard. Fucking go on!*

He let the packet go. One of those cancer sticks was going to die when they got outside.

'You can crash those fags when we get out, Paddy,' Jeni said. 'I forgot to stop off and buy some on my way over.'

Watt helped to move the man's face, his nitrile gloves gripping the hair.

'You know him, then?' Gibb said.

'He's a freelance editor.' She looked down at the book. 'I wonder why he wrote my name down?'

'I'm wondering why he was up here in the first place?'

'That other name, Amber Summers, could be the famous Indie Author,' DS Julie Stott said, coming in to the room. They all looked at her. 'Sorry for interrupting.'

'That's okay,' Jeni said. 'Tell me more.'

Julie had her notebook out. 'I spoke to the owner of this place.'

'I know... he's chasing wee lassies in Thailand.'

Julie's face started to go red. 'That's right. About him being in Thailand. He said that Foley was here alone but he'd talked about meeting up with Amber Summers, though we haven't been able to trace her yet. But her Facebook page says she's in Edinburgh, if it's the same one.'

'Track her down.' Jeni looked at Dagger. 'How long has he been dead? Give or take.'

'Not long. I'd say, around six o'clock this morning. No more than six hours.'

'Who found him?'

'The postie. He had a parcel for the owner, and the

door was wide open. He needed a signature, and rather than lump the box about with him, he knocked and entered. Found Foley like that.'

'Any chance he's good for it?'

'I wouldn't think so,' Gibb answered, 'but we're doing the usual background checks. The guy has been doing this route for years.'

'I want a full background done on Foley. Get a warrant for emails, see if we can get into his email account. Bank details. You know what I'm talking about.'

She looked at Paddy Gibb. 'Right. Outside with those fags.' She marched out of the room, hoping nobody had seen right through her lies.

NINE

'I'm nervous, Frank.' Hazel Carter looked at Miller as she parked the car. Looked in the mirror that was tucked behind the sun visor, checking her hair. 'I feel like I'm going out on a first date, not going into a psychiatric hospital to see the man I once thought was going to be my husband.'

'He's the father of your children. You'll be fine, Hazel. At least Andy Watt's not here, cracking bad jokes.'

She smiled. 'Andy's a good guy.'

'I know he is.'

'And you are too, of course.' She reached over and squeezed his hand. 'I'm so glad you made an honest woman of Kim. I thought you two were never going to get married.'

'I was just keeping my options open.'

'Pig.' She smiled and they both got out the car and walked through the lightly falling snow to the entrance of the hospital.

'Do you think I should have brought grapes or something?' she said, suddenly stopping.

'He hasn't got a broken leg, Haze.' Miller dug his hands deeper into his overcoat.

'What if his wife, Amanda, is there?' She started walking again.

'He requested to see *you*, Hazel. I somehow don't think he's going to have his wife there,' Miller said with patience. 'You'll be fine. I'll be right next to you until you tell me you want privacy.'

'I wonder what he wants. He didn't say why when he called.' She'd said the same thing to Miller what seemed like a hundred times, and each time, he didn't have the answer.

They entered the hospital, into the warmth and the smell that was unique to hospitals. They approached the reception office and gave their names. Then they were escorted upstairs to the secure ward.

Hazel stopped again. Faced Miller and put her hands on his arms. She had often thought; a different time and place and it could have been her who had carried Frank Miller's baby. But she had carried Bruce's and he had gone off and married another woman. PTSD had played a part in that but it hurt just the same.

'Promise me you won't leave me, Frank.'

Miller lifted a hand to her hair after she let his arms go. 'I'll always be here for you, Hazel. We go way back and we've been to hell and back. I will always be here for you, no matter what.'

She stretched up and kissed him on the cheek. 'Thank you.'

Miller thought for a moment she was going to say, *I love you*, but she didn't. He would have told her that he loved her too if she had.

They walked along to the nurse's station, and once again, told a nurse who they were and who they were here to see. They were buzzed through a door that was electronically unlocked, then they were in a corridor that had a security office and was staffed by male nurses. One was waiting for them.

'Hazel Carter?' he said.

'Yes. This is DI Miller.'

The nurse nodded his head. 'I'd like you to empty your pockets, please. Your valuables will be placed in a secure locker in the security room that is watched by security staff.'

Miller wondered if the man had said this so many times, it came out without him having to think about it.

They did as they were asked, putting their valuables in a little plastic bin each and a security officer took them away.

'This way,' the nurse said.

Another door was unlocked and they were in a corridor with rooms on either side.

'How is Bruce doing?' Hazel asked.

'A psychiatrist will meet with you,' the nurse said. Miller thought the man walked like he was ex-army. Maybe he moonlighted as a bouncer.

They were told to sit on a bench in the corridor and wait, like errant schoolkids waiting to see the headmaster.

'I can remember when I was in love with Bruce,' Hazel said, staring at the other wall. 'Christ, if he'd only called for backup that night, he wouldn't have ended up in a coffin and being tortured.'

'We can't turn the clock back, Hazel.' He reached over and squeezed her hand and then she held on to it, not wanting to let go. 'As much as we'd like to sometimes.'

'And that monster doing things to him at that castle,' she carried on as if she hadn't heard Miller speak. 'I know we can't change things, but I keep running it through my head.'

'Maybe you should go and speak to Harvey Levitt.' The American professor who worked for Edinburgh University and who was also the force's psychologist.

'I think he would just say the same as you, Frank.' She smiled a sad smile, and for the first time, Miller noticed the bags under her eyes and a few more lines around them.

'He'll help you. It's good to talk, and he's paid to be a good listener.'

'I'll think about it, but it's not easy with two kids.' She gently took her hand back. 'You'll know all about that now. How is Annie doing?'

Miller smiled and for a brief moment, he thought of Carol, his first wife, dead and buried, who had been pregnant with their first child when she died. His smile wavered as he thought of what had been, what road his life would have been on now had Carol lived.

'She's fantastic. I love having two little girls.'

'Once you have them, you can't believe how empty your life was before they came along, right?'

'Right. I wouldn't swap this for the world.' He looked up and saw a man staring at them a few doors along. An older man in a tweed jacket, wearing an open-necked plaid shirt. His glasses were down his nose a bit and he smiled as he peered over them.

'Inspector Miller and Ms Carter. I'm Doctor Delfs. If you'd like to come into my office.'

They stood up. Miller felt himself sweat and loosened his overcoat. He took the scarf from around his neck and stuck it in his pocket. They walked towards the old man, who seemed more like an eccentric uncle than a psychiatrist.

He ushered them into his office and they stood for a moment. A kettle was sitting on a side table with the usual suspects lined up; a jar of coffee, a bag of sugar with a spoon sticking up out of it. Some little plastic cups with milk in them.

'Coffee?' he asked pleasantly as if this was what they had come round for.

'Thanks,' Miller answered. 'With two of those little cups of milk.'

Hazel said she'd have the same.

'Please, have a seat.'

They sat on the leather couch, which had a table in front of it. Miller wondered if this and the desk were to give the doc a fighting chance if he had anybody in here who had more than a cup of Nescafe on his mind, and the psychiatrist came over with the cups. 'Only one of them has poison in it,' he said with a smile.

Miller swapped them round. Grinned at Hazel.

'Well, now I guess you know which one of us has self-preservation mode already switched on,' she said to the doc.

Miller sipped some coffee, which tasted surprisingly good.

'I put it in Detective Carter's,' he replied. He took his own coffee and sat behind his desk, leaning back, putting his feet up on the table. 'Do excuse me, but my sciatica is giving me hell today.' Delfs drank some of his own coffee.

'It's not a problem,' Miller said.

Hazel started pumping her knee up and down slightly.

'Oh, please excuse my manners. Would anybody like a custard cream?'

'Look, Doctor Delfs, I'm really in a hurry here,' Hazel said. 'As much as I appreciate...'

Delfs looked at her and smiled. 'And that's what I wanted to see.'

'What?'

'I wanted to see how long it would be for your patience to run out.' He held up a hand even although Hazel hadn't said anything. He was just cutting her off at the pass. 'If Bruce sees you agitated, it will make him nervous. He's doing really well and making more progress than I would have believed possible, but he's as nervous as you are, and afterwards, if you make each other nervous, *you* get to walk out. Bruce doesn't get that luxury. Not yet.'

'Do you think he'll be able to do that?' Miller said.

'Look, I can't go into all the ins and outs with you. I can only do that with his wife.' He looked at Hazel. 'I'm sorry about that. I heard what happened of course, but I have to be straight with you. What I can tell you is, he's making good progress. As to the possibility of him getting out, you would have to ask his wife about that. Or him. Normally, doctor-patient confidentiality kicks in, but in here, we have to have regular meetings with a spouse so we can decide on the future.

'What I can tell you is, he's looking forward to meeting you, and he's well on the way to recovery. Those drugs that had been pumped into him have been counteracted and we're teaching him how to deal with his demons. In a different way from the way they treated him in the state hospital.'

'Can I see him now?' Hazel said.

'Yes, but I want you to go into the meeting room with confidence. Make it look like you're two friends meeting for a chat.'

'I want Frank to come in.'

'As you wish. He knows you're both here.'

'What if he tells us things about his health?' Miller said.

'Then that's entirely up to him. I think he's past the stage where he doesn't know what he's saying. But I must caution you to keep the information to yourself. We don't want any outside influence.'

'Understood.'

'Now, I'll take you along to the room and you can see him.'

They left the room and went back into the heat

of the corridor. Through another set of protected doors. Then down a corridor on their right until Delfs stopped outside a door. He knocked and entered. Stood aside while the two detectives entered.

Bruce Hagan stood up. He'd lost weight but there was a glow to him now. He'd worked on Miller's team and they'd been through a lot together and Miller felt good to see him.

The doctor left and closed the door behind him.

'Hazel, thanks for coming to see me.' He beamed a smile at her and then Hazel broke down and started crying. They held each other for a moment while Miller looked out the window through the bars in front of the plexiglass protecting the glass.

'Did he give you the lecture about not making me nervous?' Hagan said, laughing. 'He gave me the same one.'

'Oh, Bruce, I've missed you so much.'

'Me too. How are the kids?'

'They're missing their dad.'

'He obviously didn't give you the lecture about not making me feel guilty.' He smiled again as they parted.

'Oh, God, I'm sorry. I didn't mean...'

'Relax, Haze. I'm kidding. And there's Frank, staring out of the window, pretending he doesn't hear a thing.'

Miller turned round. 'Oh, are you talking to me? Sorry, I didn't hear a thing.'

He looked at the man who had turned into a raging monster and had almost killed his new-born son by throwing him off the Forth Bridge. It had been Miller who had been there and who had caught the baby. Hagan's brain had been filled with experimental drugs and they had altered his whole personality.

Now he seemed back to normal. But wasn't that the way sometimes, with people who weren't all there?

He stepped forward with his hand out to shake, half expecting Hagan to launch himself at him. But all Hagan did was shake his hand.

'That time in the state hospital was crazy,' he said as they sat down. 'if you'll pardon the pun.'

'You had it rough,' Hazel said, taking a hanky out of her pocket and wiping her eyes.

'They say things come in threes, and that was certainly true for me; first the coffin and being buried alive, then having those drugs pumped into me, and then somebody trying to kill me before I escaped from the hospital.'

'Things are going to be different now,' Hazel said. 'Have they told you if there's a possibility of, you know...'

'Getting out of here legally without me having to dreep down from the window? Yes. In fact, Amanda was here earlier in the week and we all had a sit down and a chin wag. And the upshot is, I'm going home.'

'Oh my God, Bruce, that's fantastic. When?'

'Today.'

'No! Seriously?'

He nodded. 'I've been here for months, and when they found out that I was more or less back to normal in the state hospital and they were keeping me there to use me, they did a battery of tests. I had intense therapy, and Doc Delfs and I went through so many tests. Talk after talk after talk. They did tests on me to see if I could cope and I passed every one of them.'

'You're cured, then?'

Hagan held up a hand. 'They don't use the word *cured*. I'm still on the road to recovery. There are times when I get a bit confused, but they gave me what they called a *mental toolbox*. Whenever I feel my wheels slipping, I can go into this mental box and take out the tools I need to cope. And I have to take some meds for a little while, just to relax me a little bit. But the prescription will be checked every month and I'll be weaned off it.'

'That's fantastic, mate,' Miller said.

'Don't worry, Frank, I know and understand that I'll never be a copper again. But I'll be speaking to somebody this afternoon about possibilities for employment.'

'Are you going home with...?' Hazel couldn't bring herself to say *your wife,* 'Amanda?'

Hagan looked down at the carpet for a moment. Then back to her. 'Yes. I'll be living above Tanners bar again. She still works there but she's been promoted to manager.'

'That's good. Not too far from the kids. If you still want to see them.'

'Of course I want to see them. And I promise you that when I get work, I'll help you financially. But meantime, my granny passed away and since I'm the only family she had, she left me her house. When I sell it, it will be more than enough to pay off your mortgage, have some money for the kids and leave me some left over.'

'Oh, Bruce, I'm sorry to hear that. I couldn't let you do that for me. You have a wife now.'

'We talked about it. She's fine with it. I want to do it for you after all you've been through.'

'We can talk about that later. It's more important that you're happy on the outside.'

'You make it sound like he's in prison,' Miller said.

'He is. Sort of.'

'I suppose.'

'Right then, Hazel. I have papers to sign with Amanda. Then I'll be all set for getting out. I asked you here to tell you in person.' He hugged her again. 'I'd like to see the kids for Christmas, but they said that will only be under supervision until they see how things go, but they're not really worried. I do want to get them something for Christmas though.'

'Of course you can. And I hope Amanda and I can be friends, too.'

'She'd like that, I'm sure.'

Five minutes later, Delfs came back. And they said their goodbyes.

Back in the car, with the snow coming down again, Miller looked at Hazel. He'd known her too long not to know when she was hurting inside.

'How do you feel?' he asked.

'Hollow.' And then she erupted crying again.

TEN

The flat was stinking. Last night's Chinese takeaway, body odour, and maybe some rodent decomposing somewhere. The front door pushed the mail aside.

Adrian Jackson stepped into his nephew's flat with the key he'd been given, careful where he put his shoes. He gently closed the door behind him and put the key back in his pocket. The living room was straight ahead. A quick check saw it was empty. The bathroom and kitchen too.

That left the bedroom.

Grabbing the handle as quietly as he could, Jackson turned and pushed the door open. No noise. The smell was even worse in here. Sweaty feet and God knows what else.

'Brian, ya gormless wank muffin. Get out your pit.'

A sleepy face appeared from underneath the

covers. 'Fuck off,' Brian said, squinting as Jackson opened the curtains and light streamed in. The house was cold and Jackson wondered if the electricity had been cut off.

He raised his walking stick and brought it down again and again on Brian, who yelled. Despite the duvet, the wooden shaft coming down on his hip and legs hurt.

'Up and at 'em!' Jackson shouted.

Brian slipped his bare legs out from under the cover and stood up, dressed only in underpants. 'Who the fuck are you?' he said, looking the man up and down. Long overcoat, bowler hat and a glossy walking stick. 'I haven't got the rent, so tell your boss he can f—'

Jackson lifted his cane and poked Brian in the chest with it. 'I'm not here about your rent. And put something on. You're giving me the fucking boak, standing there in your manky skids. I haven't had my breakfast yet and I don't want to be recycling anything I do have.'

Another figure roused from underneath the covers. An older woman. Jackson beamed at her. 'Mrs Mellon! How are you this very fine morning? So good to see you again!'

'Mr Jackson. I didn't know you were back in town.'

'Indeed I am. Making house calls to see some family and now, as I can see, some friends.'

'Be a love and make some coffee,' Rita Mellon said to Brian.

'You know him?' Brian said.

'I'm Adrian Jackson. Or *Uncle Adrian* as you used to call me.'

Brian's jaw dropped for a second. 'Uncle Ade?'

'In the flesh, as it were. And don't call me Ade. It annoys me, and I'm afraid I get a bit tetchy when I'm annoyed.'

'My dad said you were dead.'

'Did he now? That's something else that he and I will have to discuss. Now, do as the lady says and put the kettle on.' He looked at Rita. 'Put some clothes on. I'll be in the living room.'

Jackson chose to sit on a vinyl armchair, reasoning that there couldn't be any sort of bug, bed or otherwise, lurking about on it like there might be on the fabric of the sofa.

'Make mine black, Brian, and if you spit in it, I'll detach a certain body part that you've just been using to pleasure Mrs Mellon with.'

'I wouldn't spit in it, Uncle Ade...rian.'

'That's a good boy.' He looked at Rita as she came into the room, pulling a bathrobe round her and wearing a pair of slippers that could only be Brian's.

'Did the man in the bed next to Brian sell him those?' he said, nodding to her feet.

Rita looked puzzled. 'What?'

'Those are Brian's I assume, and they look like a pair that only a dying man would have worn in hospital.'

'It's either that or catch something off his manky carpet. I don't think he even owns a Hoover.' She sat down on the sofa.

'I told you I nearly got one in Argos, but that security guard was watching me too closely,' Brian shouted through from the kitchen.

'Eavesdropping.' Jackson shook his head. 'You certainly picked a charmer there, Rita. Does Malky know you're accepting bodily fluid donations while he's still cooped up in the Bar L?'

'I get lonely, Mr Jackson. You don't understand.' A packet of cigarettes materialised from one of the pockets in the gown.

Brian came in from the kitchen and banged the mugs down onto a coffee table, some of the hot liquid sloshing over the top onto the cheap wood surface. 'Mad Malky Mellon? He's your husband?' Brian turned pale.

'Get a cloth or something, Brian. I don't want to pick up my mug and have some erroneous drip of coffee land on my hand-stitched Italians.'

'Must be nice,' Rita said, puffing on her cigarette, nodding to Jackson's expensive shoes.

'They *are* a step up from Brian's Poundstretcher slippers, but I worked hard, Rita. Unlike your Malky, who was dumb enough to try and do the job himself, not wanting to split the money with outside contractors.'

'He was unlucky, that's all.'

'He was stupid, Rita. And there's no fixing stupid.'

Rita shrugged, the bathrobe slipping a bit, but she made no effort to fix it. Brian came back with a dirty cloth. Jackson picked up the coffee mug and his nephew wiped underneath it.

'I hope that's not the one you washed this mug with?' Jackson said, eying the coffee with suspicion.

'Of course not, Uncle Adrian.' He walked back to the kitchen and, behind Jackson's back, turned back to Rita and made a face, confirming that the cloth was indeed one he washed the mugs with.

Jackson sipped the hot liquid and screwed his face up. 'Coffee in the pen was better than this pish,' he said.

'I bet the boabys were as well,' Brian said from the kitchen, not quite under his breath.

'What?'

'Nothing.'

Jackson put the mug down. 'How is life treating you, Rita? Apart from you being forced to hang out with a wee scally like him?'

'I can't complain.'

'You working now?'

She sucked on the cigarette. 'Depends on how you define *working*.'

'As in, going to somebody's premises every day and staying there for eight hours, then getting a wee brown packet at the end of every week.'

'They don't give you wee brown packets with your wages anymore,' Brian said, coming back into the room. 'Money goes right into your bank. Unless you've ripped off a punter, then the cash is stuffed under the mattress.'

'Fucking ear-wigging into somebody else's conversation again.' Jackson looked at the young man. 'I know they put money into your bank account. You think I'm daft?'

Brian looked at his uncle like it was a trick question, so he ignored it.

'If you mean work as a wage slave, then no,' Rita said.

Jackson sat back, now unsure whether bed bugs could climb up faux leather or not, but he didn't want to stand. He put both hands on his walking stick, his bowler hat still on his head.

'Why don't you take your coat off?' Brian said.

'What, so you can rifle about in my pockets when I'm not looking?' He looked at Brian who now came round to sit on the settee.

'No, I wouldn't do that. I just meant so you can be more comfortable.'

'Comfortable? You don't even have any fucking bars running on that fire and I'm sitting here freezing my nuts off and the coffee tastes like warm cat pish.' He looked at Rita. 'And before you say anything, no, I have not tasted cat pish before, but I'm sure if I did, that instant muck would be in the same gene pool. Therefore, indeed I will not be taking my coat off. Nothing to do with the fact you're a thieving bastard.'

'I don't know what you mean,' Brian said, turning to look at Rita for confirmation that she, too, was ignorant of the charges being brought forward.

'That's a slur on his character,' she said.

'He's just done saying he tried to chorey a fucking Hoover out of Argos.'

Rita shrugged, puffing on her cigarette and blowing the smoke out.

Jackson waved a hand in front of his face. 'I gave up smoking a long time ago, Rita. When I was in Upstate Correctional, I decided to give up the little cancer sticks. Men get hooked on them, but that just makes you vulnerable. You soon start promising to do anything for them. Some guys have an arsehole like a subway tunnel, but I got word round that if there was any romantical advances upon my person, then the said suitor would find himself with a pierced eyeball, courtesy of a sharpened toothbrush.'

Rita looked at him like he was talking another language, something he'd picked up watching *The Twilight Zone*.

Jackson leaned forward a bit. 'Put the fucking cigarette out, Rita.'

'Oh. *Why didn't you just fucking say that,*' she mumbled, grinding out the ciggie in an ashtray next to her chair.

'Second-hand smoke kills,' Jackson said, watching her. 'Although maybe not as quickly as your husband would despatch my nephew there.' He knew if Rita's husband was here, he'd be stubbing the fag out on a certain part of her anatomy, just before he took an axe to Brian.

'I wish you wouldn't talk like that, Uncle Ade.'

Jackson shook his head. 'Fucking attention span of a Beagle's baw bag. I said not to call me Ade. It sounds like Aids.'

Rita chuckled. 'Say that three times, fast. *Beagle's baw bag.*' Brian joined in with the laughing.

Jackson stood up and looked at his nephew. 'Well, I'm glad I amused you. When's visiting time at the Bar L? I'm sure Malky will be pissing his pants when he finds out you've been shagging his missus.'

They both stopped laughing and Brian's face took

on a worried look once more. 'I'm sorry, Adrian, we were just having a laugh.'

'It's fucking *Uncle* Adrian, ignorant wee scrote.'

'Sit down, Adrian, please,' Rita said. 'I'm just nervous.'

'Yeah, that was nervous laughter,' Brian said.

'Against my better judgement...' He sat back down, the vinyl creaking alarmingly, sounding like he was passing gas. He moved again, just to show it was the chair.

He looked around the room before his eyes settled on Rita's. 'I'm assuming the lack of Laura Ashley furnishings means that you're strapped for cash.'

'We do alright,' Rita said.

'Why don't you tell Brian where you live? Or have you told him already?'

Rita looked unsure of herself. 'Ravelston.'

Jackson grinned. 'Ravelston Dykes. Malky Mellon and his gorgeous wife rubbed shoulders with judges and lawyers and doctors. Now it's only Mrs Mellon there on her ownsome. But I'll bet the judges and lawyers and doctors don't invite her to bingo night at the golf club along the road now, do they, Rita? They don't want to mix with the gangster's wifey while he's getting bummed in the showers over in the big house.'

'Ravelston?' Brian said. 'Ravelston? And here I am living in Muirhouse and can hardly afford a roll of bog paper, never mind a roll of wallpaper. Why didn't you tell me?'

'Why didn't you tell him, Rita?' Jackson said.

Rita looked down at the filthy carpet for a moment before looking up at Brian. 'I thought you wouldn't want to go out with me if you found out my ex is in prison.'

'Not just any old ex, Rita,' Jackson said, smiling. 'Mad Malky Mellon.'

'That too.'

'Ravelston?' Brian said, as if repeating the fact would make it more real.

'Get over it, Brian,' Jackson said. 'In fact, I moved in to Ravelston today. My good lady procured a quintessential pied-a-terre in an upper enclave in this very fine metropole, not a stone's throw from your lady friend.'

Brian looked sideways at Rita. 'Don't look at me,' she whispered. 'He's either talking Klingon or he's having a stroke.'

'Neither, my lovely Rita. But I do happen to know that you have some sort of financial woes.'

'I'm behind on the mortgage if that's what you mean.'

'Indeed I do. My sources tell me that you're not far off having the house taken away.'

'You told me you rented a flat in Gorgie,' Brian said.

'Shut up, Brian,' Rita said. 'Yes, that's correct,' she said to Jackson.

'Then I may have the solution to your problems.'

'Oh yeah? Do tell,' she said, her voice laced with sarcasm.

'It's that little word we just mentioned, Rita, one that some people add the word *shy* to at the end.'

'Work.'

'Exactly. Like my fine nephew here. A quick call to his mother procured me the information that he neither seeks the aforementioned word or has had much success with it when he has managed to weasel his way through a job interview. What say you, Brian?'

Brian shook his head. 'Ravelston?'

'For fuck's sake, we've moved on from that,' Jackson said, resisting the temptation to batter his nephew with the walking stick.

'What was the question again?'

'Would you like to make some money? Both of you.'

'Yes,' Brian said.

'Depends on what it is,' Rita said, this time, her tone laced with suspicion.

'It's not having your expensive gaff taken away from you, it's not having your little hairdresser's

Mercedes taken away from you, it's not having to fire your housekeeper, it's not having to get your next pair of knickers from Oxfam. If you still wear any.'

'Mercedes?' Brian said. 'I can barely afford a bus pass.'

'Don't go on, love,' Rita said, taking the packet of cigarettes out of her pocket, then putting them back when Jackson gave her a look.

'Are you in, Rita?' Jackson said, standing up again.

'I'm in.'

'Me too,' Brian said.

'I'll be in touch,' Jackson said, getting Brian to write down his phone number. Then he walked out of the living room and down the hall.

'A housekeeper?' he heard Brian say as he closed the front door behind him.

ELEVEN

'Money always goes to money, even when you're a crooked bastard,' Paddy Gibb said as the car pulled into the side of the road on the North Bridge.

'There's Frank there,' Andy Watt said, turning the engine off.

'Skulking about in the doorway like a union conspirator.' He opened the door and a bitter wind cut into the car.

'Why aren't you waiting inside?' he asked Miller, who was standing stamping his feet with his hands dug into his overcoat.

'I thought I saw Carol's sister go inside.' Venus Molloy was Carol's sister, a woman his dead wife didn't know about until close to her death. She wasn't just Carol's sister, but her twin. It made Miller's stomach churn just looking at her. Not because she wasn't a beautiful woman, but it was like looking at a ghost.

'Let's get inside and see how much hassle this cockbag gives us,' Watt said as they entered the hotel.

Inside, the hotel was superb. Robert Molloy hadn't spared any expense.

They approached the reception counter, bypassing the restaurant entrance.

'Swanky,' Watt said.

'Can I help you, sir?' the receptionist asked.

'We're here to see Robert Molloy,' Gibb said.

'A bit out of your price range, sergeant,' Molloy said, coming down the marble staircase. 'I'm expecting these fine examples of modern policing in Edinburgh,' he said in the direction of the receptionist.

The three detectives turned towards Molloy.

'You look like some kind of laird, standing there,' Gibb said.

'And you look like a bunch of pheasant pluckers. Try saying that when you're pished. Come away up, see my new office.'

They followed the man like he was the Pied Piper until they came to the next level. Inside, the office was three times as large as the one in his club in George Street. Michael Molloy was waiting, sitting on a couch.

'Here comes the posse,' Robert said, holding the door open for the detectives.

'Pussy, more like,' Michael said, almost under his breath.

'Shut up,' Robert said.

Miller looked around, glad that Venus wasn't there, but just as he sighed a breath of relief, she walked in. He felt as though a jolt of electricity had passed through him as he looked at what could have been his dead wife.

'Hello again, Frank,' she said, smiling.

'Hi.' Jesus, her mannerisms, her looks, the sound of her voice. If Miller didn't know better, he would have thought this was actually Carol.

'How's the new addition to the family?' she asked.

'Couldn't be better. Thanks.'

She smiled at him.

'Right lads, what can we do for you?' Robert said, offering them a seat.

Venus poured them coffee which they accepted.

'It's regarding the writers' conference you have going on,' Gibb said. '*Capital Crimes*.'

'It's not illegal to put on some artsy-fartsy thing, is it?' Michael said.

'Excuse my son's acerbic tone once more,' Robert said. 'Go on.'

'Someone was found dead this morning. Murdered,' Miller said, looking at Venus out the corner of his eye. 'We believe he was connected with the writers' conference.'

'Well, I'm off,' Michael said, getting up. 'And I was with my girlfriend all night if you want my alibi,' he said, and with that, he departed the office.

'I'll give you her number,' Robert said. 'Who was this person?'

'We're not at liberty to give out names, but it seems he was connected to somebody here at the hotel. Amber Summers. She was part of the show,' Gibb said, not sure if it was technically a show, or a conference or some sort of meeting.

'The seminar, Chief Inspector? It's not a circus we're hosting.'

'Seminar. Whatever. We're going to need a list of names.'

Robert looked over to his daughter and she flitted out of the room like a ghost. 'Venus will look up the name for you. I couldn't find my way around a computer with a guide dog and a Sherpa. But what do you think of the new gaff?'

'You've certainly come up in the world, Molloy,' Miller said.

'It was an expensive wee beastie and no mistake, but it will be worth every penny. Officially opening on Christmas Eve, although we're already open.'

'Seems a bit small potatoes, having a wee literary fest in your place,' Andy Watt said.

'It might seem like that to an uneducated sloth like yourself, sergeant, but it generates free publicity. There are reporters sniffing about as if we put some bodies behind the new walls.'

The three detectives were silent.

'I'm kidding. Of course, we wouldn't put any bodies in the walls.'

Venus came back, from her own office, Miller presumed. It had been a surprise to learn that she had accepted a job from her father. Molloy had only recently found out that she was his daughter, and Venus had said she didn't want anything from Molloy. But Robert Molloy was a very persuasive man.

She came across and handed Robert the sheets of paper she'd had printed out.

'It seems we do indeed have an Amber Summers staying here. Checked-in late yesterday afternoon. Staying for this little soirée and checking out on Sunday.'

'Have you met her?' Miller said.

'Yes, I did as a matter of fact.'

'So, you didn't need that piece of paper to tell you she was staying here,' Watt said. 'As usual, it's just a charade.'

Robert said nothing for a moment. Then he handed the papers to Gibb.

Gibb looked at them then looked at Watt like a headmaster would look at the school bully.

'Please tell your sergeant what it says,' Robert said.

'It's a list of people who are booked in for the seminar. They're registered as attendees because they got a discount. The other sheet lists the times that Ms Summers' key card was used for her room.'

'My daughter can liaise with security staff to have the CCTV checked if you can give us a timeframe.'

Gibb hated asking Molloy for help but knew there was no other choice. 'Make it from four am until ten am for a start.' He looked at the piece of paper. It showed that Amber Summers had checked into her room the night before and hadn't left until ten that morning.

'I'll get onto it. Anything else?'

'Do you know if she's in the hotel just now?'

'She was, as of half an hour ago. I spoke to her myself.'

'Is there any way this could be faked?' Miller said, pointing to the papers. 'Could she leave her room somehow without anybody knowing? I mean, key cards just register the door being unlocked, don't they?'

'I suppose. The cards just unlock the door.'

'We'd like to go and talk to her,' Gibb said.

'I'll have somebody go and find her, if she's still in the building.'

They all stood and followed Robert back to the lobby. 'If you would like to wait in the lounge, I'll have somebody bring her to you. If she's not here, we'll let you know, and I can have somebody call you when she comes back,' Robert turned and walked away leaving the detectives to make their way into the lounge. It was done up like a room in a baronial castle.

'I wouldn't mind bringing Jean here,' Watt said.

'That would look good to Standards. They would think you're in Molloy's pocket.'

'I said I'd like to, but I wouldn't. I don't want to make Molloy any richer than he already is.'

'We're going to have to ask if there's somewhere private,' Gibb said, seeing a few people milling about.

'True, we don't want to give them a free show,' Watt said, wondering if there was any chance of a free coffee.

Venus Molloy appeared at the entrance to the lounge and motioned for Miller to come to her.

She took him outside into a quiet spot in the hotel lobby.

'Did you find her?' he asked.

'Yes. She was in the spa. I've told her some police officers want a chat. She's one of the organisers of the seminar. But before you speak to her, I'd like a quick word, Frank.'

Miller could feel his cheeks getting hot again. He asked himself, *What would Kim say if she walked in right now and saw you talking to your dead wife's twin sister?* He'd be fucked.

'Okay.' He was going to add, *I'm all ears* but he was sure that by the colour of them, she was already well aware of his ears.

'I know I gave you the runaround a few months ago, and I'm sorry for that. I was scared. I just don't want you to think I'm some kind of fool.'

'Don't worry about it.' He looked at her for a moment. 'I didn't know you were working for your dad.'

'He kept asking me to join the family business. I make triple what I was making before, and he treats me like a princess.'

'What about Michael? How does he treat you?'

'Michael's... opinionated at times, but he's warming up to me.'

'They can be a tough family.'

'I know.' She reached out and gently squeezed his arm. 'I'm really excited for you and Kim. How would she feel about me buying a gift for the baby?'

'I'm sure she would be fine with it.'

'Good. Here's my number. Give me a call late next

week. Give me a chance to go out and buy something. Then you can come and pick it up.' She took out her mobile phone and looked up her number before rattling it off. 'I won't ask for yours. I don't want things to get awkward for you and Kim.'

He added her number under *contact*. Would he lie and tell Kim it was one of his informants if she saw it? He honestly didn't know. He didn't see it as a big deal, but Kim might.

'You and your colleagues can use my office if you'd like somewhere private to talk to Amber Summers.'

'That would be great, thanks. I'll just go and get my boss.' He walked away and motioned for the other two detectives to follow him. Venus showed them to her office along a little corridor from the reception area.

'I'll bring her in,' she said, smiling at them, and closed the door on her way out.

'She's nice,' Gibb said.

'She's too young for you,' Watt said. 'Better sticking to old Maggie Parks.'

'Shut up, for God's sake. And since when did you stop calling me *sir*?'

'Easy there, *sir*. I'm just saying. What with your fragile ticker and Venus being at least thirty years younger than you.'

'Twenty, son, not thirty.'

'Whatever. Same diff. You're better sticking to Parks. Two creaky old coffin dodgers.'

'I'm not much older than you, cheeky bastard.'

Watt laughed. 'I can actually see your blood pressure elevating as we speak.'

'You'd like that, eh? Me popping my clogs in front of you. Give you something to gossip about in the canteen. Well, here's a newsflash, I'm not going anywhere soon. It will take a lot more than high blood pressure to finish me off. I'm going to stick around as long as I can just to piss you off.'

'Now, now, Paddy, where would you get the idea that you piss me off?'

'It's *sir*. Bas—' Just then, there was a knock at the door and Venus entered with a woman who appeared to be in her thirties.

'I was expecting some old boot,' Watt said under his breath.

'Shut up, ya bloody heathen,' Gibb said, brushing past Watt and holding his hand out. 'I'm DCI Gibb, Police Scotland. This is DI Miller and DS Watt. We'd like to have a word with you.'

'Oh, my Scottish fan club, all in one room. I seem to have moved up from having to use a phone box,' she said, smiling.

Miller had imagined her as being in her sixties,

wearing some flowing, flowery dress, but this woman was young and dressed in jeans and a polo neck.

'I'll get somebody to get another couple of chairs,' Venus said.

'Don't bother,' Gibb said, 'those two can just stand. Thanks anyway.'

'Anything else?'

'Some coffee and a plate of Jammy Dodgers wouldn't go amiss,' Watt said, and he got the feeling she wanted to tell him to fuck off, but she was too polite. Give it time.

Venus left, and Gibb parked himself behind the desk, indicating for Amber to sit down on the chair opposite.

'I'm assuming that you're not here to help me with research or are part of the seminar,' she said.

'You're right,' Gibb said, while the other two stood at the side of the desk by the window that looked out over the station below. 'We need to ask you a few questions about a man named Lee Foley.'

Her demeanour changed. 'Foley?'

'You know him?' Miller said.

'Yes, I had the misfortune to get acquainted with him.'

'In what way?' Watt said.

'Don't make it sound mucky, sergeant,' Amber said,

the highlights of her cheeks turning rosy, as if she'd been outside for a brisk walk.

'I was just meaning...?' He left the sentence unfinished, both of them knowing exactly what he was inferring.

'I'm not sure if you read books, any of you, and I'm not saying that I am ultra-famous, but I do alright. I'm sort of well-known in indie publishing circles. I organised this weekend seminar for budding writers.'

'On your own?'

'Myself and a few other writers. We want to give back to the writing community.'

'How do you know Foley?' Gibb said, feeling the conversation was going off at a tangent.

'He's a freelance editor. I contacted him a few years back. Before I was so well-known. And he edited my first few books. He made a lot of mistakes, but he was cheap and sometimes we writers have to go down that road until the money starts to come in. But he was an absolute swine. Has he been at it again?'

'At what?' Gibb said, leaning forward as if he was giving somebody an interview for a job.

'His cheating, lying, scumbag ways.'

'Could you clarify?'

'He was a little weasel. He edited my first few books which was fine, then he got the next one in the series, and then he sent me an email demanding more money.'

'More money for what?' Watt said.

'He said that he had put his prices up and he had sent me an email telling me this a few months previously. He was a lying bastard, of course. I kept every email from the little tosser, and there was no such thing.'

'Did he have the new prices on his website?' Miller said.

She looked at him. 'You would think. But his website was down.'

'You didn't give him extra money?'

'Indeed I did not. I mean, it's not as if he was a fabulous editor to begin with. He was hardly worth the money he charged, never mind paying him more. He kept my money and he kept my book.'

'How did you pay him?'

'Through PayPal.'

'Couldn't you get your money back?'

'I launched a dispute, but it doesn't cover transactions for digital goods. He won, basically. Little smartarse.'

Gibb leaned forward on the desk. 'It would be safe to say that you harboured a grudge against him.'

'No, it wouldn't be safe to say. Yes, I hate the little bastard, but what's done is done. All I can say is, I wouldn't give him a recommendation to any up-and-coming author. It's one of the subjects we'll be touching on this weekend.' She took a deep breath and let it out slowly, as if she had got everything off her chest that she wanted to say. 'Why all the questions about him? Has he made a complaint against me? If so, let me tell you—'

'He's dead. He was murdered in the house he was renting in Edinburgh.'

'Murdered? Amber smiled. 'I can't say I'm surprised. He was an evil little fuck.'

Gibb raised his eyebrows and took a quick look at Miller, who shrugged.

'No sympathy card to his wife, then?'

'I don't think even his wife stuck around for long.'

'How do you know that?' Watt asked.

'You would have to understand how the weasel operated to know that.'

'Help us understand,' Gibb said, sitting back.

'He started off professionally. Then he started talking personal stuff. Like how his wife was cheating on him. And they were getting a divorce and how much of a bitch she was. And how he would like to *throw the fucking bitch into a river with a boulder tied to her*. His words, not mine.'

'Do you know his wife's name?'

'No, but she was a nutter, according to him.'

'He confided in you, I assume?' Miller said.

'He would tell me these things. All about his personal life. It was just in conversation. Run of the mill stuff, until he touched on the subject of his wife. Then it was poison.'

'Did he have any family?'

'Not that I know of. Just her. His third wife.'

'Can you tell us where you were between four o'clock this morning and seven o'clock?' Gibb said.

'Here in the hotel. In bed.'

Gibb nodded, knowing that was corroborated by the printout from the hotel. 'I'll need the names of the organisers who are here with you. Do you know if any of them had dealings with Foley?'

'We're all indie authors, but I know they all use different editors. We spoke about using freelancers and the risk we take putting our work into the hands of strangers.'

Gibb stood up. 'Thank you for your time, Miss Summers. If we need to speak to you again, we know where to find you.'

Amber Summers stood up and smiled at Gibb. 'I hope the bastard died in pain.'

TWELVE

The offices were in Castle Street, between Princes Street and George Street. The Scottish Adoption Agency.

Lou Purcell stood and looked up the steps to the building door. It was shared by an employment agency too. He wished he had asked his friend along. He and Matt went back a long way and Matt was the only one who had kept in touch when Lou had moved to Aberdeen.

Now he was here on his own, feeling like a nervous schoolboy.

He took a breath and climbed the stone steps, entering the warmth of what was once a tenement building where people lived until the greedy developers got their hands on it and divided it into commercial property.

He walked up a flight of stairs and went into the office. It smelled musty, like nothing had been dusted for a while. 'I'm Lou Purcell,' he said to the young receptionist. 'I have an appointment.'

She smiled at him. He noticed her squint teeth and looked away quickly when she looked back at him. Scottish dentistry at its finest.

'Mrs MacLeod will see you shortly.'

He looked at her for a moment, thinking she had called him *shorty*, but she went back to what she'd been doing before he interrupted her. There was a chair to one side, implying that he should sit in it, but he stood around like a bogus gasman.

A woman appeared from the hallway behind the desk and smiled at him. 'Mr Purcell?'

'That's me.'

'Follow me, please.' She turned and walked ahead of him and stopped to indicate which office he should go into.

'I have some of the information that you asked for,' she said when they were both seated.

'That was quick. I thought it would take much longer,' he said.

'Sometimes it does, sometimes it doesn't. You were lucky.' She opened a folder on her desk and rifled through some papers before looking at him. 'I have to say; most people decide to look for their parents at a younger age.'

'I just recently found a note from my deceased mother, tucked away with some other papers.'

'And your adopted mother never spoke of this before?'

'No, she never mentioned it. As I said, I just found it by accident.'

'How old are you now, if I may?'

He told her.

'As you can imagine, the adoption was a very long time ago.'

I'm not a fucking hundred, Lou thought but kept his smile on. He had no words to add to that.

'These are the details I managed to get. Your biological mother, Lucille, worked as a housemaid for a large family. The head of the household was Thomas Young. He was a judge. Your mother was sent off to live in what can only be described as a house for unwed mothers, run by a group of nuns. You were then born in the Simpson Memorial Maternity Pavilion.'

'Wouldn't I have known that from my birth certificate? About my father?'

'You would have been given an amended certificate which would have had your adopted name on it, with your birth details. It wouldn't have said anything about you being adopted.'

'Oh, right.'

'When your mother came to these offices, it was noted that she was alone, and she didn't want the father's name put on the birth certificate.'

'It's no wonder. He'd had his way with her, and then shirked his responsibilities.'

'It was different times back then, Mr Purcell.'

'I know that, but still. If he had acted responsibly, he would have owned up to what he had done and had his name on the certificate. At least my mother told me his name, thank God.'

'I can't make any comment on that. I'm just here to help people trace their biological parents.'

'Well, he was married with kids, and was making decent money and had a responsible job. No wonder he didn't want to upset the apple cart.'

'I can give you a letter to take along to the Sheriff court. They have some items on hand that you can look at. Unfortunately, you can't take them away, but you can certainly look at them.'

'I'll do that. My adopted mother said that he had kids, and I'm assuming that she got the information correct, and if so, how do I go about tracing them, or relatives of theirs?'

'I will caution you, that can be a very upsetting thing for them. To find out that the man you love, or loved, had a child with another woman. It can shatter the memories they have of their father. It can even destroy some families.'

'I'm sure my biological mother wasn't too thrilled to have been put in a home with nuns. I'll bet the judge's *real* family didn't have to endure that.'

'Quite. But I would tread lightly, Mr Purcell. As we don't have any formal information on your father, that is something you would have to try and do yourself with the help of the family tree service you told me you had tried.'

'Okay. I'll try them. But if the judge was from Edinburgh, there have to be some connections somewhere. Some old addresses or something. I'll get somebody on to it.' He stood up, the woman starting to annoy him.

Mrs MacLeod handed him an envelope with the letter inside. 'They'll help you at the courthouse.'

'Thank you.' He paused for a moment before speaking again. 'You must deal with a lot of people trying to find their families. Do you think there's any chance any good comes out of contacting a family member who didn't know you existed?'

'Never,' she said, matter-of-factly.

THIRTEEN

The Tollhouse bar on Old Dalkeith Road had seen better days. Adrian Jackson stood outside it after getting out of the taxi, looking at the faded sign above the window and door.

It had been a very long time since he had been in any bar never mind one that he owned, but that was about to be remedied.

He went in the front door and the pungent odour of last night's spilt beer hit his nostrils. The few patrons in the bar who were drinking stopped to look in his direction. One of them sniggered and nudged his friend.

Jackson walked forward, his shiny new cane tapping on the floor. The air was thick with cigarette smoke. The older bloke who had laughed lit up another cigarette and blew the smoke into the air.

'There's no smoking in pubs nowadays, I believe,' Jackson said, walking over to stand beside the man.

'Is that right, Grandpa?'

'Aye, what the fuck's it to you?' his friend said, all sign of laughter now gone.

'That's enough of that,' the barman said, coming round the counter. 'If the smoke annoys you, piss off to some other fancy hole.' He stood in front of Jackson, looking like he was about to touch his jacket.

'I'm new here,' Jackson said to the punter, ignoring the barman.

'Well, you better fuck off as my pal says. You're not going to last long in here.'

'Is that right?'

'Aye, it is,' the man said, standing up.

'Well, I think I'll last a lot longer than you, son. Get out. You're barred.'

That brought a round of laughter.

In the twenty-five years Jackson had been in prison, he had been in a few fights, more in the early days when some of the tough gang members had tried it on, but he had a lot to prove, so he didn't waste any time getting wired in. If nothing else, prison had sharpened his reflexes. When the younger man turned his head to look at his other friends laughing, Jackson knew a punch was coming.

When the man wound up his arm and swung it,

Jackson was already stepping sideways. He brought his walking cane up, grabbed it with his left hand and deflected the man's punch, catching his arm and pushing down, bending the man over. Then he brought his cane round and battered it at high speed into the man's shins. The man screamed just as Jackson stepped back and swung the cane into the man's face, breaking his nose.

This took only a matter of seconds, and then Jackson saw the barman coming for him. Jackson lifted the cane and pointed it towards the man's face.

'One more step and I'll break your fucking jaw with this.'

The barman stopped.

'Get that fucking twat out of here. I meant what I said; he's barred.'

'Who are you?' the barman said, confusion on his face.

'The owner.'

'Yeah, right.'

Then a man came out of a small corridor at the end of the bar. 'What's going on here?' he shouted, his Irish accent strong. 'Christ, Mr Jackson.' He looked at the barman. 'What the hell are you doing? That's Mr Jackson, the owner. Fucking eejit.'

'Oh, I thought he was joking.'

Jackson lowered his cane and smiled. 'Now we've

got that sorted, do what you're paid to do, son, and get that fucker out of here. And Sonny, make sure he never sets foot in my property again.'

The manager nodded. 'You heard him, get that shitehouse out of here.'

The barman grabbed hold of the troublemaker and hauled him out of the door and threw him into the street. His friend followed, cursing Jackson as he left.

'Anybody else got a complaint?' Jackson asked. Nobody said a word. 'If I catch any of you fuckers smoking in my pub again, I'll have you lit up. And please don't make the mistake of thinking that's an idle threat.'

Cigarettes were hastily stubbed out in response.

'Come this way, Mr Jackson, and I'll get you a wee nip,' Sonny Henderson said, ushering Jackson through to the back office. Like the rest of the pub, it was dark and dingy.

'Jesus, Sonny, this place has gone downhill.'

'Times are tough,' the manager said, pulling a bottle from the drawer in his desk.

'Put that away. I don't drink anymore.'

'Ha ha. You own a bar and don't drink.'

'I've spent the past twenty-five years banged up. Do you think we had a piss-up every Friday night?'

'No, sorry.'

'Now that I'm back, I want to start showing an

interest in my pubs. There was a time when I didn't think I'd see the inside of one of my boozers again.'

'I've been here for a long time, Mr Jackson. I've seen them come and go, but I've done me best to hold on to the place.'

'My wife has done me proud, no doubt.'

'I was hoping you would come home, Mr Jackson. I told Mrs Jackson that when you came home – *when* mind, not *if* – when you came home, I would retire.'

'Don't you like working for me?' he asked.

'Oh yes, don't get me wrong, I do enjoy working for ye, but there are some aspects of the job that are maybe not as joysome.'

'Like what?' Jackson was sitting with his hands on the cane.

Sonny sat down, the old chair behind his desk creaking. 'This fooking chair creaks just about as much as me. Bastard thing lost a nut a long time ago and it's never been the same since. See, down there, a big fooking—'

'Sonny! You're fucking havering now. Shut your piehole and tell me what's really going on.'

The old Irishman looked at his watch. 'You sure you want to be here right now?'

There was a knock on the door and before Sonny could speak, the barman poked his head in. 'They're here. And they're saying it was short last week, so you owe them another hundred on top.'

Sonny jumped up out of his chair. 'Ye fucking eejit. Why didn't you send me a text or something?'

'Or something? What? Smoke signals?'

'Get out, ye loud mouth wee fuck.'

The barman retreated and Jackson looked right at the Irishman. 'What's going on?'

'Ach, for fuck's sake. You were bound to find out soon enough. We're getting ripped off.'

'Define *ripped off*.'

'Protection.'

'Ah.' Jackson stood up and went to stand behind the door. A few moments later and the door opened.

'Sonny, ye wee Irish fuck. Did that halfwit you call a barman tell you that you were short last week?'

'No, but he told me,' Jackson said, slamming the door shut. Both the men turned round to look at him.

'Well, who do we have here?'

'Let's just say, your little scheme to con me out of money just hit the buffers.'

The men looked at each other. 'Oh dear. I think you just made a big mistake, old man. Now you and that Irish fuck are going to have to go up the road to the Royal to have some stitches seen to, while we stay here and wreck your bar.'

The second man pulled out a Stanley knife and

grinned, but Jackson had seen the hand go into the pocket and he was already twisting the top off his cane. He drew the slim sword out in one swift movement and sliced it across the first man's face, causing a jet of blood to fire through the air from the rent in his cheek. He screamed and put a hand to his face just as Jackson put the tip of the blade to the other man's throat.

'Put that fucking knife away, son, or else this is going to go into your jugular, and when I say I will make you both disappear, you better believe it. I'll have you both buried so deep, not even a pig would sniff you out with a truffle stuck up your arse. You got that?'

The first one leaned against the desk while the second replied in the affirmative, scared that if he spoke too loudly, the shiny metal would slice into his neck.

'I'm going to ask you a question and you're going to answer truthfully the first time, or I am going to take this sword and cut your dick off. Again, I don't make idle threats. Who do you work for?'

'Peter Stanton,' the man said without hesitation.

'Stanton? That useless wanker?' He took the sword down and put it back into the cane. 'Tell him that Adrian Jackson is back in town, and he will be making house calls. Every penny that he's taken out of this bar, I want it back. Every fucking penny.'

'I'll tell him.'

Jackson looked at the office door. 'Right lads!'

The door opened and four men came in. They were bulked up like they'd just come from the gym. 'Get these pieces of shite out of here.'

Sonny stood with his mouth open as the two thugs were bundled out by two of the men while the other two stood just outside.

'Surprised, Sonny? Don't be. Fiona told me all about them. I told her to keep on paying the money until I got out. I told her I would sort Stanton out, and I will. I'm going to get in his face and tell him it was a bad idea to fuck me over.'

'Jesus, that was magnificent. I was scared of those bastards, let me tell you.'

'That's why you wanted to retire?'

'It is indeed.'

'You're not retiring. I'm going to turn this place around and you're going to be at the helm. Only this time, with a hefty pay rise. I might only have some manky boozers left, but all that is going to change. And there's going to be some blood spilt along the way.'

FOURTEEN

There were six names in total, written in Lee Foley's notebook. Five of them were at the writing seminar, including Amber Summers. The other four were also writers.

Friday evening was a *getting to know you all* affair, before the two days of lectures and exercises. The writers and tutors were in a corner of the bar when Miller and Purcell walked in with Steffi Walker and Julie Stott.

'We won't keep you long, but we need to talk to you about Lee Foley,' Purcell said.

'Can't you come back later?' one man said. 'I mean, this is important to us.'

'We can talk to you up at the station,' Miller said. 'It's just round the corner and it shouldn't take more than two or three hours, by the time we get an interview room sorted and get the ball rolling.'

'Shut up, Isaac,' a woman said.

'You know each other?' Purcell said to her. 'Miss...?'

'Constance Britain. *The* Constance Britain.'

'I'm sorry, what?'

'I'm the writer, in case you were confusing me with the other Miss Britain.'

'Right.'

'Anyway,' Miller continued, 'the manager of the hotel has said we can use a conference room to interview each of you if that would be more convenient for you.'

Venus Molloy came into the bar and smiled at Miller. She had changed into black jeans and an open-necked shirt but still looked incredible. He had to keep reminding himself that it wasn't Carol, but her sister.

'I'll show you where the room is,' she said to Miller. He got up and followed her out into the lobby and down another corridor. Through a door and into a small conference room, which had a table with chairs round it.

'This is a small room, obviously, but we have bigger ones. My dad wants all sizes of groups to be able to come to the hotel.'

'It's a nice place.'

She put a hand on his arm. 'I miss her too, Frank. Carol. We had just gotten to know each other when it was taken away from me.'

'I know, I've moved on in my life, but I'll always have a place in my heart for Carol.'

'I know. If you ever feel like popping round and having a chat about her, feel free.'

'Do you still live in Fife?'

'No, I've moved over here now. I have an apartment over at Quartermile.'

'How does Molloy feel about this?' he said with a smile.

'You are family, Frank. That's how I see you and my dad understands that. I wish I'd gotten to know you better a lot sooner. But I mean it; if you want to talk, I'm not that far from where you live.'

'Message received and understood.' There were a few seconds awkward silence. 'I'll go and get the first one.' He walked away, feeling his guts upside down again. It was like talking to the ghost of his dead wife, dredging up memories of her that he would prefer to have been kept at bay. He thought of her at times, like when one of her favourite tunes came on the radio, or a particular cooking smell hit his nostrils, but he didn't want to sit down with her twin sister and swap war stories.

He had Kim now, and the baby and a stepdaughter.

It was called *moving on* and he was fine with that. He thought that Venus would get more out of it than he would.

'The room's ready, sir,' he said to Purcell.

The superintendent looked at the faces, each of them looking like they were going to be taken outside and shot in the back of the head.

'I'll go first, if you have no objection,' Constance Britain said.

'Is this part of the course?' a man said. 'If it is, it's pretty good. I'm impressed.'

Purcell walked over to him. 'No, it is not part of your course. This is for real. A man's been murdered and we're going to find out who did it. And you lot are the main suspects.'

The man beamed. 'Super! He's almost like a real police officer.' He turned to another man sitting next to him. 'My mother said I shouldn't waste money on this, but isn't she the one who's going to be eating her words?'

'For fuck's sake,' Purcell said under his breath to Miller. 'It's going to be a long night.'

'Should I be coming in with Constance?' another man said.

'And you are?' Purcell said.

'Anthony Robson. Tony. A fellow writer and friend.'

'You her lawyer, Tony?'

'No.'

'Then, no you can't come in with her. Sit and wait your turn.'

Purcell and Miller escorted Constance Britain along to the make-shift interview room.

'You look a bit young for a copper,' a voice said behind Steffi Walker. She turned to look at him. A man, sitting in a wheelchair.

'Doctors, coppers, we all look young to…'

'Older people,' he said. 'I'm a little bit older than you. I'm Paul, husband of *the* Constance Britain. She insists I say it that way when I talk about her.' He smiled and held his hand out.

'DC Steffi Walker.' She shook hands with him. 'Your name's not on our list, is it?'

'Not as far as I'm aware. I've never met the man before. Constance is the writer in the house.'

'You're not here in a writing capacity then?'

'Sort of. I dabble. I've almost finished my own book, so she wanted me to come along and mix with other like-minded people. Constance is one of the writers who's putting this show on. She's an indie, like Amber, but her books are soaring up the charts. She sees it as her way of giving back. Me? I give back by donating my old sweaters to the Oxfam shop.'

'Where do you come from?'

'Birmingham, originally. We live in a small village just outside now. Not too much of a drive, but it's peaceful.'

'How long are you up here for?'

'We're heading back home just before Christmas.'

'You have family there?'

'No. Constance and I have been married before, and we don't have kids. We'd talked about it before this happened,' he said, looking at the wheelchair.

'How long have you been together?' Steffi pulled a chair up and sat opposite Paul.

'Ten years now. We'd been going together for a year before we got married, then the crash happened just before our first anniversary.'

'I'm sorry to hear that.'

He took a sip of the pint he had on the table. 'Don't be. If you sit around feeling sorry for yourself, then life's over. I try and keep upbeat, although it's hard sometimes.'

'What sort of books does Constance write?'

'Crime thrillers. Set in London. She goes down there often, doing research and I think it's paid off. Now she's in Edinburgh, her character is going to come up here and he gets involved with some murder. Talk about art imitating life.' He drank some more lager, almost swallowing the glass. 'Maybe she can use this as research.'

'Is this old rascal bothering you, detective,' Anthony Robson said, coming up behind Paul and putting a hand on one of the chair's handles.

Paul turned round. 'Tony. Just in time. I believe it's your round. And get the lovely Steffi here a wee nip.'

Wee nip didn't quite sound right coming with a Brum accent.

'I'm fine, thanks.' She put up a hand.

'Come on. Tell her, Tony. This poor lass is stuck in here with us, working, while she should be getting ready to go out on the town. This is Friday night. You should be going out to the dancing.' He made a back-and-forward motion with his arms, imitating dancing.

'If that's how you dance, no wonder you used to go home alone on a Friday night,' Robson said, laughing, and slapping Paul on the shoulder.

'Before I met Constance, I could get any woman I wanted. Now I'm in a chair, it's become more of a challenge.'

'You're a married man. There should be no such thing as a challenge.'

'You know what I mean.'

'I do that, my friend. I'm not disabled and even I can't get a woman.'

'You're plug ugly though, that doesn't help.'

Robson laughed. 'Cheeky sod. Another pint?'

'Cheers, mate.'

Robson walked over to the bar to get the drinks in.

'Do you two know each other or did you just meet up here?'

'Me and Tony have known each other for a few years. His wife was in group therapy like me. Learning how to deal with your disability without jumping off a bridge. She was very nice. I liked her a lot, but the poor thing had a massive heart attack and passed away. I met Tony when he used to pick his wife up and we hit it off. Same with Constance, and she doesn't really get on with anybody. But we've been friends ever since. Constance told him about this gig and suggested he come along for a break. And to be honest, he's my drinking buddy. The only one who stuck around.'

'True friends are hard to find.'

'You better believe it. He's a great guy. Nothing is ever too much for him. If I'm struggling with something, he's right there, helping me.'

'Is that you talking about me?' Anthony said, coming back over with two pints. 'My ears are burning.'

'I'm just telling this detective here that you're usually a tight arse when it comes to getting a round in.'

Robson laughed. 'Listen to him. The last time he bought a round, he got a shilling in his change.'

Steffi smiled. 'Do you do any writing, Mr Robson?'

'I'm trying. Constance is helping me craft my first novel. Mainly I just came up to help young Paul here.'

'You're too modest. When it's finished, I'm sure it will be a bestseller.'

Robson looked at Steffi. 'I can only hope. I just need to get the mechanics of writing sorted and then we'll see.'

Paul looked at Steffi. 'I've read it and it's superb.'

'Only with Constance's help. I wouldn't have known where to start otherwise.'

'If anybody can help him on the road to success, it's my wife,' Paul said, smiling.

'What kind of books do you write?' Purcell asked.

'Maybe you're expecting me to say, *Flowery Romance,* but I write crime thrillers. Gritty noir, where a lot of blood is shed.' Constance Britain sat back in the chair and looked at Purcell like she wanted to fight.

'Women are the best crime writers,' Miller said.

'Too right we are. It used to be a male-dominated world, but with the explosion of indie writers, we proved to the world that women can write good crime fiction.'

'Agatha Christie was a good crime writer too,' Purcell said.

'Well, she was one of the lucky ones. I'm talking about nowadays, when indies have much harder work to do than the *Big Five* authors.'

'We got you in here to ask you about Lee Foley,' Miller said, 'not to get you wound up about publishing.'

'I'm sorry, but it's a subject dear to my heart. Nobody understands what a job it is to get your books noticed. It's bloody hard work.'

'That's why you need a good editor,' Purcell said.

'Yes. Lee Foley didn't fall into that category though. You get what you pay for. I used him, then found a better editor who charged more money, but he was far superior to Foley.'

'Do you know why he was in Edinburgh? Was his name on the attendees list?'

'I have no idea, and no, his name wasn't on that list. But the seminar has been widely publicised and considering he swims in these waters, he was bound to find out about it. It wouldn't surprise me if he was touting for business. And since it's being held here in the hotel, it's a public pace, so there's nothing to stop him creeping about here.'

Except Robert Molloy's bouncers Miller thought.

'He had a list of names in a notebook that included yours and others who are giving lectures. Do you know why?'

Constance spread her hands. 'How would I know? I haven't had contact with him for a while. Maybe six months or more. He wrote to me asking me to reconsider taking him on. I laughed at him of course. He couldn't edit a grocery list.'

'Do you know anybody who would want to kill him?' Miller tapped a pen on a notepad.

'Take your pick. I'm sure he ripped off a lot of writers. It doesn't surprise me that he's dead. What does surprise me is nobody murdered him sooner.'

FIFTEEN

Percy Purcell fell onto his leather recliner and let out a deep breath.

'Hard day?' Suzy said.

'As always. Interviewing a bunch of writers who have put on some kind of weekend get-together where they can tell the great unwashed about how they made it big without somebody holding their hands.'

'Indie publishing is a big thing nowadays. Like that woman, what's her name again? Her that's married to the thriller writer.'

'Dawn Rutherford.' Purcell said.

'Yes, that's her. She writes good stuff. She self-publishes and she's doing really well. I've read some of her books.'

'I understand that, but this woman I interviewed

tonight had a voice like a foghorn. She can clear a room just by walking into it. Face like a bulldog.'

'Percy, that's not nice.'

'I'm not in a *giving a compliment* mood.'

'Would you like a beer?'

'No, you sit down and I'll get you one.' He got back up and walked into the kitchen.

'And a massage too?' she shouted through to him.

'That's just taking advantage. Next, you'll want me to take off all your clothes and—'

'Easy, Christ,' Lou said, coming out of the bathroom. 'Do you always act like that in front of visitors?'

'For God's sake. I thought Friday night was staying in night with Elizabeth and comparing arse cream?'

'Listen to yourself. One day when you've got piles, you'll think about me.'

'Yeah, 'cause you're both a pain in the arse. Get it?'

'You're the only one laughing.'

'My talent's wasted on you two.'

'Percy, behave, for goodness sake,' Suzy said. 'Your dad came round to see you.'

Percy handed the beer bottle to his wife. 'What? You had a change of heart and you've decided not to cut me out of your will.'

'Nope. You're still getting nowt.'

'Would you like a beer, Lou?' Suzy said.

'No thanks, love. I'd better be getting home.'

'Have a beer, you anti-social wee fa—'

'Percy!' Suzy sat up straighter in her chair.

'I was going to say *father*.'

'You lie like a bloody rug,' Lou said.

'Listen, why don't you hang fire and I'll get showered and you can come with me up to Tanner's bar?'

'You paying?'

'Of course. You haven't broken that ten-bob note yet, and I wouldn't want you to spoil the world record.'

'Welcome home!' Amanda Hagan said, throwing her arms round her husband's shoulders.

They were in the living room above the pub in Juniper Green. Hagan hadn't seen the inside of this place for a long time.

'I still can't believe this is happening.' He held onto her. 'After all that's happened to me, I don't understand why I'm not in a box for real.'

'Don't be talking like that, love. All that stuff that went on wasn't your fault.'

'I know. As long as I stay on the meds while I go to therapy, I'll be fine.'

'Did they tell you if you'll be seeing Jill White or not?'

'I will be. The last time, I gave her the runaround,

but I wasn't thinking straight. Now I'm on the right track and I will be able to talk to her properly this time.'

They sat down at the dining table. Amanda suddenly looked sad.

'What's wrong?' Hagan asked.

'You married me instead of marrying Hazel, but that was when you weren't thinking clearly.' She lifted her head and looked at him. 'Now that things aren't so foggy, what's stopping you just leaving and going back to her?'

Hagan was silent for a moment. 'Hazel and I were together for a short while. I never knew Jane was my daughter. I fell in love with the wee thing, and then when we had Daniel, that was magic. But then life decided to deal me a crap hand, and things went the way they did. However, through all the fog, and the anger and frustration, I held onto the fact that you were my wife. Whatever feelings I had for Hazel, they're gone. I told Hazel about my granny's house and she didn't want that, but I want to help her and the kids.'

'It's the right thing to do.'

'I'll see the kids, but as for any feelings I had for Hazel, there's nothing there.'

'I know it sounds selfish, but I fell in love with you, Bruce, and you're my husband. I want it to stay that way.'

'It will. I promise you.'

'Let's go downstairs and celebrate.'

'I have to stay off the hooligan juice.'

'You can have an orange then. I'm going to have a bottle of Bud.'

'You don't think any of the regulars will find it funny I'm back here?'

'If they make any wisecracks, they're out on their arse. But this is Friday, so the place will be jumping later.'

Then her phone rang.

'This place is out of the way, isn't it?' Lou Purcell said to his son.

'It's hardly the set for *The Hills Have Eyes*. Although you would make a good extra on that. No make-up needed.'

'Shut your hole. Get your hand in your pocket. And make mine a double.'

'Steady there, cowboy. I don't want to be pouring you into a Joe Maxi after a couple of swallies.'

'I thought they had a wee disco thing going on here at one time?'

'Fucked if I know. It wasn't one of my regular haunts.'

'I bet it's jumping, being a Friday.'

'Just be on your best behaviour. No trying to pick up some young lassie and getting us into a fight or something.'

'I have been in a pub before. How do you think I ended up marrying your mother?'

'Because her parents wouldn't pay the ransom.'

'Always a smartarse.'

Even wearing casual shirt and trousers, Percy still looked like a cop. Some of the regulars didn't make eye contact.

'Help you?' the bartender asked him.

'I'd like to speak to Amanda Hagan.' He showed his warrant card.

'I'll call her.' He got on the phone and spoke before hanging up. 'She'll be right down. Can I get you drink meantime?'

'Two bottles of Becks.'

'I'll have the same,' Lou said, grinning.

The barman got the beer and put the bottles on the counter.

'I'll get those,' a woman's voice said from behind them.

Percy turned to see Amanda Hagan. 'Cheers. This is my dad, Lou.'

'Why don't you come upstairs. Bruce is there. I'm assuming that's who you're here to see?'

'I was going to ask you if it was okay.'

'Of course it is. He'll be pleased to see you.'

Percy turned to Lou. 'I won't be long.'

'Lou can come too. Bruce will be happy to see people again. He's spent a lot of time on his own.'

'Okay.'

They followed her through to the back corridor where the entrance up to the flat above was.

Upstairs, Bruce was standing in the middle of the living room, smiling, holding a glass in his hand. Orange juice.

'This is a nice surprise, sir,' he said, raising his glass. 'Who's your friend?'

'This is my dad, Lou. We're just having a drink.'

'Good to meet you, son,' Lou said, shaking Hagan's hand.

'You're looking good,' Percy said.

'I'm getting there. Still on the road, but I can see the end now.'

'Please, sit down,' Amanda said.

Percy and Lou sat on the couch while Hagan took one of the chairs. The living room was big and well kept.

'Did you come round to the pub to check up on me?' Hagan said, putting his glass down on a table.

'No, nothing like that. I knew we went through some tough times when you were going through things. I just wanted to come here to offer you some support. If there's anything you need, just give me a call. And don't call me *sir*.'

Hagan looked down for a moment. 'I don't have to call you *sir* because I'm no longer a police officer and never will be again.'

'I'm not going to sit here and give you some spiel. We both know that what happened to you wasn't your fault, so I've been in talks with Jeni Bridge, and she is going to take it higher. We think you're entitled to a pension. Your federation rep will be calling you. He and I sat down and we went through the fine details, but I don't see that there will be any problems. Everything that happened to you in the first instance was while you were on duty. That will be enough to give you the pension, as those later actions were a direct result of an active investigation you were part of.'

Hagan looked at him. 'I don't know what to say.'

'You don't have to say anything. Just make sure you go to see Jill White and take any meds they give you so you can look after this lady of yours.'

'She's the one looking after me.'

'I heard you were a good copper,' Lou said. 'I hope you don't mind, but my son filled me in on what happened. You deserve to be looked after.'

'That's good enough of you to say that, Lou. To be honest, I was just happy to be transferred to the Royal Scottish. They've helped me tremendously.'

Lou drank from his bottle. 'What are you planning on doing with yourself now?'

'I'm going to play it by ear, for now, Lou. If you see what I mean.' Hagan moved his long hair to one side to show the older man what remained of one of his ears. He picked up his glass and took a drink of the juice. He made no attempt to hide the fact that some of his fingers were missing on one hand and one of his ears had been cut off.

'What is it you do yourself, Lou?'

'I'm a retired bank manager. Right now, I'm doing some family research.'

'That keeps you out of mischief.'

'For now. I'll find some trouble to get myself into no doubt.'

Hagan raised his glass. 'Here's to us.'

Lou clinked his beer bottle against the glass, quite pleased with the way things had turned out. He would later tell his son that he was glad Hagan hadn't greeted them in his living room, wielding a chain saw.

SIXTEEN

'Relax, Peter. You'll give yourself a stroke.' Chrissie Green stood behind Peter Stanton as he stood looking out of her living room window. Across The Meadows, where the lights were on, lighting up the pathways, enticing pedestrians with a false sense of security.

Stanton chugged back the whisky and handed the crystal glass to Chrissie for a refill. She held up her own glass in one hand and a cigarette in the other. He walked over to her drinks cabinet and poured himself another.

'I can't believe that bastard,' he said, putting the crystal stopper back in the decanter. 'Taking on two of my men like that.' He turned to face his girlfriend. 'First day back in town and he goes picking a fight.'

'He's just flexing his muscles, like he's some bigshot. It'll blow over.'

'It'll blow over? Is that all you've got?'

She slowly took the cigarette out of her mouth and blew the smoke into the room. 'I beg your pardon?'

Stanton took a deep breath. 'All I'm saying is—'

'I beg your pardon?' she said again.

He held a hand up. 'I'm sorry. I'm just raging right now.'

'I don't want you to confuse me with your ex-wife, Peter. All I ask for is a little respect.'

'Of course. I'm sorry.'

She smiled and walked over to him and kissed him on the cheek. 'You always promised me you would treat me as your equal, that's why I'm so good at my job. But don't start talking to me like you spoke to her.'

'I'm sorry.' He rubbed a hand over her cheek.

'I'm your right-hand woman and your lover. Two out of three ain't bad.'

'I know. I should think myself lucky that you're still by my side. Even though I don't get to see you as much as I'd like these days.'

'We have each other. I don't spend the night with you, but we do things that matter. We show each other love in other ways. Besides, it won't be for long.'

'God, I love you, Chrissie.'

'I know you do.'

He looked like a little schoolboy who had lost his ball. 'It wouldn't kill you to say it back sometimes.'

'And if I fall in love with you, I *will* say it back.'

'You can love somebody without being *in love* with them.'

'I'm not your mother, Peter. I don't console you when you've fallen and hurt your knee.'

'You're saying that you don't love me?'

Chrissie sighed and tried to take the glass away from him, but he swiped it sideways and finished the contents before handing her the glass. He smiled.

'You're like a child.'

'I know.' He wiped his mouth with the back of his hand.

'How is Adrian Jackson ever going to take you seriously if you're stoating about like your legs are made of rubber?'

'Fuck 'im.'

'Since when are we using that kind of language in front of a lady?'

Stanton looked sheepishly at her. 'Sorry.'

She smiled at him and reached out to stroke his cheek. 'Peter, we can't let the Adrian Jackson's of this world get to us. He's just another bump in the road.'

'I know, you're right. But I have to make sure he doesn't cause trouble.'

'He's already started causing trouble. And you shouldn't have sent men into his places to get money. I told you so.'

'What was the difference? He was in prison in America.'

'And now he's back in Edinburgh. And he wants his money back. Are you going to give it to him?'

'Oh, I'm going to give it to him alright.'

Peter Stanton grabbed his jacket from the back of a chair and stormed out of her apartment.

'Is it not my turn for driving?' Scramble said from the passenger side.

'I'm sure it is, but I'm also sure I don't want the fire brigade cutting me out of the fucking car.' The hatchback sank down alarmingly as Larry got in behind the wheel.

'Fuck me, it's about to tip over.'

'Don't talk shite.' He slammed the door a little too hard.

'Is that shut right?'

'Fuck off. At least I can drive like my arse is on fire if we have to leave a scene quickly.'

'Christ, one of those bicycle cops could catch us in this poofy thing. Why don't you just paint it pink and hang furry dice from the mirror while you're at it?'

'Will you stop whining like an old fanny. You're

doing my tits in.' He started the car up and put the demister on.

'And next time, get something that has heated seats.'

'Anything else? Something that will wipe your arse, maybe?'

'I'm fucking freezing. Maybe we could get a Land Rover. The army sell off their old ones. We could invest in one of those. I've always fancied booting about in one of them.'

'Yeah, 'cause the army fit their motors with heated seats. You'd be lucky if you could wind the windows up by hand.'

Larry pulled out of their driveway from the back of the house. The car was black. Not red, like Scramble wanted, but something that could sit in a darkened street without sticking out. Scramble had conceded the point.

'What are we doing for Christmas dinner?' Larry asked.

'I wish you wouldn't talk like we're a bloody couple.'

'There's nothing wrong with that nowadays. Not like in my old man's time.'

'Well, good for you, but this boy right here is a well-oiled love-making machine, ladies membership only.'

'What? Pish. Well-oiled machine.' Scramble put

his hands in front of the heater vent in a vain attempt to keep the circulation going. 'Besides, if we've nothing else on, we have to think about what we're having for Christmas dinner. We work together, we live together. Just a couple of heterosexual pals having a scran together.'

'As long as you let me do the cooking,' Larry said. 'I don't want the fucking house burnt down.'

'I want you to surprise me on Christmas,' Larry said, heading up towards the A70 so they could hit the Edinburgh City Bypass.

'Well, I'm getting you fuck all, so that should be a surprise.'

'You know how this is going to go, don't you? We'll go out for our staff Christmas party, which is you and me, and we'll end up getting blootered, and you'll have to help me into a fast black and take me home. Then I'll puke, feel like shite and then on Christmas Day, we'll eat turkey and fall asleep.'

'Sounds like a bundle of fun. I wish I had a regular girlfriend sometimes.'

'And how would you explain what you do for a living?'

'I'd have to give this up, wee man.'

They drove round the Calder roundabout and hit the bypass.

'Larry, we spent years in the army together. You

learn to do without a woman long-term, with the occasional foray into the wild to keep you going. We have a good life, don't we?'

Larry smiled in the dark. 'Yeah. Being married twice should have taught me a lesson.'

'That's it! My wife was just a nag. Bumping into you in a pub one night was the best night of my life. We get paid good money. It's far better than working in an office or bouncing on a door.'

'I know. And to be honest, I fucking enjoy this.'

'I know you do, mad bastard.'

They both laughed.

Newington was an upmarket area of Edinburgh, to the south of the city centre. Glenorchy Road was upper class, filled with semi-detached Victorian properties. The house they were looking for was on the right as they came in from the Mentone Terrace street.

'Nice gaffs round here,' Larry said. 'I wouldn't mind living here.'

'Can you imagine what the neighbours would say when they found out what we did for a living?'

'They would show us some respect.'

'As they waved us off after we were taken away by the law.'

Larry knew they couldn't drive up and down the street more than once. It was his experience that people in enclaves like this would have a sixth sense when it came to cars trawling up and down their street and they would be straight on the phone to the police to report suspicious activity. And since this was a classy neighbourhood, the filth would turn out just to keep the taxpayers happy.

He had looked at the address on Google Street View and knew exactly where they were going. He parked up the road from the house. It was late, but not too late that it would look suspicious for two men to be walking about. Timing was everything.

They parked and walked back down to the house. It was surrounded at the front by what looked like a ten-foot hedge, with a door shape cut into it. They couldn't see the house from here unless they looked through the entrance. Which, Larry supposed, was the whole point.

It was what you wanted when you were an accountant for a gangster.

Their remit was to make it look like a hit. Not an accidental fall down the stairs, but somebody sending a message.

They wore suits with shirts and ties. Had gloves on, and overcoats with woollen hats. Winter hits were always easier because you could walk about with layers of clothing on without raising suspicion.

The old man lived alone, no housekeeper, his wife having been dead for several years. He had one adult daughter who lived in London. He was retired from his regular job and was now employed in a nefarious capacity.

Larry knocked on the door. They waited. The old codger was probably in bed. They had been supplied with a phone number, just in case.

But they saw a light come on in the hallway. A tall, lanky figure coming to the door behind the frosted glass. It opened, jarring on a chain.

Larry held up the warrant card. 'DCI Williams. Can we come in and speak to you, sir?'

'You can speak to my lawyer.' Edward Hopkins was about to close the door.

'It's about your daughter, sir. We have some bad news. Can we come in?'

The door closed and they heard the chain being slid along. Larry smirked at Scramble before the door was opened fully and the old man let them step inside.

'Come through to the drawing room,' Hopkins said.

'Fucking drawing room,' Larry said, shoving the old man, who went staggering into the room. 'Why can't you just call it a living room like every other daft bastard?'

Hopkins whirled round. 'Who are you? What do you want?'

'He catches on quick,' Scramble said, taking the hat off. 'Sit down. We need to talk to you.'

Hopkins looked between both men. 'I knew you weren't police officers.'

'Why'd you let us in then?' Larry pushed the man again and the edge of the chair caught him behind the knees and he fell heavily into the heavily padded cushion.

'You've been a naughty boy,' Larry said.

'How dare you come in here and talk to me like that.'

Larry looked at Scramble. 'How dare us.'

Scramble laughed. He looked at the expensive antiques in the drawing room, thinking that no doubt there was more expensive stuff lying about the house. They made it a rule to never take anything, that way it couldn't be traced back to a hit.

'Nice things you have,' Scramble said.

'Take what you want and leave. At my age, I don't need any of it.'

'We're not here to steal from you,' Larry said.

'Then why are you here?'

It became apparent when Larry pulled out the silenced gun.

'Oh no, please. I don't know who sent you, but I can pay you double.'

'We have to send a message to somebody, and that means you have to die. Sorry, old chum, nothing personal. It's just business.'

'Wait, I can—'

Larry fired and the bullet caught Edward Hopkins in the forehead, throwing his frail body backwards. He slumped in the chair. Larry stepped forward and put another bullet in the old man's heart.

SEVENTEEN

Frank Miller was looking down into his new baby daughter's crib, watching her breathe, getting older with each passing second. He knew Carol would have thought she was beautiful. Annie Miller. He wondered if she would go on to do great things with her life.

'She's beautiful, isn't she?' Kim said, coming into the room and putting her head on Miller's shoulder.

'Just like her mum,' he said, putting an arm around her. 'I'm so glad we got married.'

'Oh me too, Miller.' She laughed and kissed him on the cheek. 'Come on, let's get some breakfast. Before little miss wakes up and wants feeding again.'

His stepdaughter, Emma, was still in bed.

'You know, since the girls are sleeping, we could… you know…'

'My father warned me about you,' said Kim. 'I should have listened, but oh no, I fell for your charm.'

'I'm just putting the idea out there. Purely for your benefit.'

'I'll stick to toast and coffee, thank you very much.'

'Millions of women around the world would kill for a piece of this.'

'Yet, you're mine and off limits,' said Kim.

'It's an exclusive club, you're the only member, and yet you refuse to use the facilities.'

'Tonight's Saturday night, so we'll see. And hey, it's not even your birthday.'

'And it's Christmas next week. There *is* a God.'

She laughed as he went through to the kitchen to put the kettle on. Not even nine o'clock on a Saturday morning. He remembered the days when he would lie in until one o'clock in the afternoon.

Charlie, their cat, came running into the kitchen, looking for his bowl to be filled. He had been Carol's cat. She had picked him out at the animal shelter in Balerno. He had been a kitten and had run over to her as if he knew he wanted to go home with them. He had chosen his new mummy. Miller petted the cat, rubbing his head, then he poured cat food into a bowl.

There was a knock on the door. He answered it and his father's girlfriend was standing there. They both lived along the hallway from him. Samantha Willis, the crime writer.

'I'm sorry to disturb you, Frank,' she said.

'No, don't be daft. We're up. Did you seriously expect us to be having a lie in now?' He smiled at her and stepped to one side, letting her in. Kim was standing in the hallway.

'Hi, Sam. What's up?'

'You heard about the murder of the editor, I assume, Kim?' she said.

'Frank kept me in the loop.'

'I just got a call from one of the writers who organised the seminar. I agreed to give a talk about the mechanics of writing, but my friend just sent me a text.'

For a moment, Miller focused on her American accent before he paid attention to what she was actually saying. 'Is there a problem?'

'You could say that. One of the writers has gone missing.'

'Who told you this?'

'Constance Britain,' said Samantha.' They were going to meet for breakfast at eight-thirty this morning, and they all appeared, except a woman called Amber Summers. They got a staff member to check up on her and her room hadn't been slept in. There's been no activity on her key card since last night. They were all in the bar, having a drink, when Amber said she was going up to her room. She never went up apparently.'

'They tried calling her mobile phone, I assume.'

'Yes, they tried. Her phone was left in her room.'

'Really? That's a big no-no right there. Who leaves their phone in their room?'

'Jack said we should at least report it. The others don't know what to do. Yes, they're writers and wannabe writers, but they're not sure what they can do in Edinburgh.'

'I'll come down and talk to them,' Miller said.

'I'll come too. Jack is already down there, poking about. I had to remind him he's a retired cop, not an active one.'

'My dad won't listen. It's in his blood. Let me get my coat.' He turned to Kim. 'You'll be okay with our daughters?'

'Of course I will. This isn't my first kick at motherhood.'

He kissed her and left with Samantha, going downstairs and into the sharp cold. It had snowed through the night and the pavements were slick.

There was a buzz of activity in the hotel. Venus Molloy was trying to placate a few irate writers.

'If you can all please settle down, we'll try our best to find out where your friend is.' She looked round and saw Miller approaching. 'In fact, here's the police now.'

The writers turned to Miller. Venus mouthed *sorry* to him and he gave a gentle shake of his head. *Don't worry about it.*

'One of our organisers has gone missing,' Constance Britain said, walking up to him. Her husband, Paul, was at the back of the pack, being pushed in his wheelchair by Anthony Robson.

Miller held up a hand. 'Okay, I'm going to need you all to be quiet. I'll talk to you, Mrs Britain, and we'll go from there.'

'The breakfast room is open,' Venus said. 'I'll have coffee and rolls sent in.'

'Thank you. Now, if you'll come with me,' he said to Mrs Britain. He and Samantha walked with the woman into the breakfast room. She seemed more annoyed than distraught.

'I hope that cow isn't doing this as a publicity stunt,' she said, sitting down.

'I thought you and Amber were friends?' Samantha said.

'Friends? That's a bit of a push, dear. Acquaintances, maybe, but not friends.'

'I didn't get that impression from you yesterday,' Miller said, hanging his coat on the back of a chair as a waiter brought some bacon rolls and coffee over to them.

'Compliments of Ms Molloy,' he said.

Miller looked at the rolls, wondering if he should have one, then decided that he wasn't here in an official capacity and tucked into one. Samantha did, too. Mrs Britain refused.

'I need a ciggie more than anything,' she said.

'Mrs Britain, there's nothing we can do about a missing person over the age of eighteen until they've been missing for at least twenty-four hours. Technically. But I can speed up that process. However, I have to warn you, if this *is* some kind of publicity stunt, charges can be brought against her.'

'Listen, if that bitch has done this as a stunt, you won't have to worry about charges being brought. There are people here who would be lining up to slap the cow.'

'I'm sensing hostility here when everybody thought she was the bee's knees yesterday.' Miller washed the roll down with some coffee.

'Amber Summers thinks she's the best author since Shakespeare. Yes, she sells a lot of books, but there are a ton of writers out there who write better stuff and don't get noticed.'

Sour grapes, Miller thought, but kept it to himself.

Then he saw Jack, his father, himself a retired detective, coming into the room with Robert Molloy.

'There's no sign of the woman,' Jack said. 'She was

seen leaving the hotel last night around seven-thirty and there's no sign of her coming back.'

Molloy looked like he wanted to punch somebody. 'The hotel isn't fully booked yet. More guests start arriving Sunday night, after this caper is over.'

'Who are you?' Mrs Britain said.

Molloy stared at her for a few seconds, and Miller wondered if he was going to let loose on her. 'I'm the owner of this hotel. I heard what's going on.'

'We don't know where she went to. We knew Edinburgh was a rough city, and there's a lot of tourists here, but we didn't think for a million years that one of our group would go missing.'

'You lot are crime writers, and nobody could imagine something like this happening?' He looked at Jack. 'Keep me in the loop, Jack. Some snoop from *The Caledonian* is coming round to talk to them today and that's all I need, somebody to be missing. And I better not find out that it's somebody's idea of a game.'

'It's no game. At least not that I'm aware of.'

'Tell me about the last time you saw her last night,' Miller said.

'We were in the bar, and she said she was going up to her room. The rest of us wanted to go out and explore the city.'

'You all went out in a group?'

'No. I went with my husband, and we walked

down to Princes Street Gardens to see the Christmas market down there. The others, well, you'd have to ask them.'

They heard voices outside the restaurant and then Andy Watt appeared with Hazel Carter. 'Kim said you were here. We got a shout, sir,' Watt said. 'Just up the road.'

Miller nodded, knowing better than to ask what it was in front of the others, but it was obviously serious.

Outside in the hotel reception, he shrugged his coat back on. 'Give me a rundown.'

'The corpse of a man has been found in his house,' Hazel said. 'Shot to death.'

EIGHTEEN

'Christ, are you trying to make your heart explode?' Scramble said, walking into the kitchen.

Larry was standing at the cooker, frying what seemed like every item in the fridge.

'Killing makes me hungry. What can I say?'

'You really need to invest in a treadmill or something. Your ticker is already protesting.'

'Pish. I'll diet in the new year.'

'Fucking die, more like.'

'Morbid bastard. I mean, what kind of talk is that a week before Christmas?'

'Just don't follow it up with a chocolate doughnut.'

'You want some?'

'Of course I do.' He shrugged off his overcoat. His face was red. 'We really need another car. That old jalopy is a piece of crap.'

'It doesn't stick out.'

'I'm not saying we should get one that sticks out more than a leper, but get something that heats up quickly. Not like the diesel pish.'

'It's a well-known fact that diesels don't warm up until they've been running a while.'

'I want one with remote start and heated seats.'

'A huge thing.' Larry handed Scramble a plate full of food.

'Ta.' Scramble dug in.

Larry shovelled food onto his own plate. 'You know why they buy those things? They go off-road in them. Off-road and park on the pavement.'

They both laughed. He sat down opposite his friend.

'To be honest, we could do with one of them Land Rovers. And no, I don't mean the ex-army things, I mean a Discovery with all the bells and whistles. We've got the money to buy one.'

'And when we're done this week, we'll be able to buy one each.'

'So, what are we waiting for then? Let's go and look at them today. The dealer is only up the road.'

Larry nodded his head. 'You know something? I think you're right. For a change.'

'Compliments indeed. Oh, that reminds me,'

Scramble said, 'that old radge was about to put the mail through the door. Smiled at me, he did.'

'Maybe you're his type. Nothing wrong with that. Ask him out for Christmas.'

'Fuck off.'

Scramble laughed as he went through the pile of mail then slid the letter across the table to Larry. 'Look at the postmark and the return address.'

'Looking at my fucking mail now?'

'It's right there. Besides Happy Harry pointed it out. He's hinting for a Christmas card.'

Larry looked at him. 'Wait; he pointed out my ex's address?'

'I just said so, didn't I?'

'Fuck. He's certainly trying to take an interest. Maybe we should give him an early Christmas present.'

'That's what I was thinking. Maybe find out where he lives and break one of his knees so he'll be taken off his round.' Scramble laughed.

'Good idea,' Larry said, eating round a piece of sausage.

'I'm kidding.' He looked at his friend to see if he too was kidding, but he wasn't. 'What's the rule of thumb? Don't draw attention to ourselves.'

'It's not like we would do it on the doorstep. It

would be when he was out. Make it look like a mugging.'

'You're not serious?'

'I am fucking serious, Scramble. The last thing we need is some old sweetie wife peaking in through the windows, seeing if we have his tin of shortbread wrapped up yet.'

'Seeing you going about in your manky Y's would be enough to put him off.'

'If we think the postie is going to be a problem, we need to take care of that problem,' said Larry.

'You really think this could go sideways?'

'Look at it this way, he's angling for a gift, which they all do, but now he's seen my ex's address, and that could be the starting point for a conversation. He's not really interested who she is, of course, but he might just use that as an excuse to start talking to you, and then before you know it, you've explained the whole situation; we're both divorced, living in the same house because we're contract killers. It's the small things that get people caught.'

Scramble ate some bacon and egg. Washed it down with coffee. 'I think you might have a point. I'll make a call, get some info on him, then we can decide what we want to do about him. Aren't you going to open your letter?'

'So you can neb at it. Keep your filthy mitts off it.'

'We'll keep an eye on things. Meantime, we've got a busy time ahead of us. That wasn't just one hit we're getting paid for.' Scramble took a piece of paper out of his pocket and put it on the table. 'There's another four. Two of them are normals, but two are specials. If we take them, then the fee is tripled for each one.'

'Triple? Somebody must be desperate.'

'That's not for us to decide. We know the risks. Triple payments are few and far between, but they have triple the risk.'

'I think we should take them,' said Larry. 'Let our handler know we'll do it. If you're in, that is.'

'I'm in. I want a bloody new Land Rover and one hit will pay for it.'

'Good. When you call him back, tell him they'll be done. Where are the jobs?'

'All local.'

Larry ate some more. 'After we're finished, we can go away for a break in the sun.'

'Agreed.'

Larry looked at the list of four names. Two were highlighted in yellow, people whose deaths would have to look like accidents. He looked at the last name. 'I wonder who Frank Miller is?'

NINETEEN

Jeni Bridge paced back and forth in her kitchen. Coffee or wine? She thought. It was only breakfast time, but she felt like she needed a kick. Alcohol or caffeine?

The doorbell rang. Coffee it was.

She answered it. 'Thanks for coming.'

Percy Purcell stepped over the threshold, out of the cold and into the heat. He was dressed in black jeans and an overcoat, with a black sweater underneath.

'Let me take that for you.'

He took his coat off and unwrapped the scarf from his neck. Stamped his boots on the mat, depositing some snow.

'Go through to the kitchen. I have some coffee on.'

'I've never been here before.'

She looked puzzled.

'I don't know where your kitchen is.'

'Sorry. Straight ahead.'

She hung the coat on a hook in the hall and followed him through to the kitchen. 'You know we don't stand on ceremony in a social situation, Percy. Call me Jeni.'

'It sounded urgent,' he said, looking around. The Keurig stopped dripping, so she took the mug out and added another K cup.

'It's French Vanilla,' she said, putting the mug on the counter. She took milk out of the fridge and was about to pour when she put the carton down and stood hunched over the counter, her shoulders shaking.

'Jesus, Jeni, French Vanilla is fine,' he said, walking over to her.

She turned to look at him and tried to smile but failed miserably. She broke down and flung her arms around him.

Purcell held onto her, not knowing what else to do. After a couple of minutes, she pulled away from him.

'Oh, what a stupid old bint. Go on, say it.'

'I'll say nothing of the sort,' he said, seeing a box of tissues on the counter. He pulled one out and gave it to her. 'Why don't you tell me what's wrong?' He poured the milk and left the carton for Jeni. When her coffee was made, they sat down at the dining table.

'I've been stupid, Percy. I've *done* something stupid.'

'Haven't we all?'

'You don't understand. It's why Lee Foley had my name written in his notebook.'

Purcell put up a hand. 'Shouldn't you be telling this to Standards?'

'I already had my interview with them. You know how it goes; I'm the commander of Police Scotland Edinburgh Division, but I was still made to feel like a wee lassie. I didn't have much time for DI Harry McNeil when he was with Standards, but the guy who replaced him is a total prick. I am under instructions to stay away from that case, not to discuss it with anybody in any way, shape or form.'

'And yet you have me over, discussing that very case.' He sipped the coffee which tasted very good.

'That's the problem.'

'Christ, don't tell me you offed him?'

'You think I got you over here to confess before you lead me away in handcuffs?'

'No, I don't think you're that silly, Jeni.'

'Good. Because I didn't kill him. But I might know why somebody else did.'

TWENTY

'Ravelston,' Brian said, stepping into Adrian Jackson's hallway.

Jackson put a hand on his nephew's chest. 'Get your fucking boots off, baw bag. I don't want you traipsing all kinds of shite on the new shag.'

'Sorry.' Brian started undoing the laces.

'Talking of shags, where's Rita Mellon? You know, Mad Malky Mellon's missus.'

'She went in a right fucking huff after your visit yesterday. She thinks that I think she's been using me.'

'Christ, you must be some fucking machine, boy. I mean, you haven't exactly got yourself a palace down there in Muirhouse land.'

'I thought she was some old scrubber looking for a toy boy. I mean, she's not averse to putting her hand in her pocket, but I didn't realise she had a silk purse.' Brian walked into the living room.

'Old scrubber? Dearie me, but you do have a way with the ladies.'

'She said she'll be along shortly, so she can't be that much in a huff. Besides, she's curious to know what work you want us to do. That way she can make her next mortgage payment and keep her house.'

'Don't be so sceptical. I was exaggerating. She's at least three months away from moving in with you.'

'That will be right. She moves in and then Mad Malky hears about it and suddenly I'm being fed through a wood chipper.' He walked over to the window and looked out onto the snow-covered gardens out front, next to the private car park. 'Where's Fiona?'

'It's fucking Aunt Fiona. Fuck's sake, I've been back five minutes and all I get is a show of disrespect.'

'Sorry. Where's Aunt Fiona?'

'Never you mind, nosy bastard. She's away out doing something, if you must know. Sit down though. When Rita gets here. I want to go over some stuff.'

'It will be good to be doing some work for a change. Not filling shelves in Tesco, but real work.'

'Illegal stuff, you mean?'

Brian smiled. 'Yeah, illegal stuff.'

Jackson took a couple of swift strides over to his nephew and grabbed him by the hair. 'Never let me hear you talk like that again. What I do has not to be talked about to anybody. Hear me?'

'Yes.'

Jackson let Brian's hair go and pushed him by the head. His heart was beating like a jackhammer. He hadn't had to move that fast since some Rastafarian had tried to make him lick a part of his body that Jackson had no intention of licking. And the said Rastafarian had to eat his meals through a straw for several weeks afterwards.

The doorbell rang. Jackson stood in the middle of the living room while Brian stood next to the window.

'Go and see if that's our delightful Rita, pal,' Jackson said.

First you pull my hair and now I'm your fucking pal, Brian mumbled, but he went to the door anyway.

'What's wrong, lover? You look like you've been crying,' Jackson heard Rita say.

'I've not been crying. I was just yawning and it made my eyes water.'

'Well, you can come back to my place tonight and I'll make your eyes water.'

They came into the living room. Jackson was holding up a decanter for Rita. 'A little drop to warm you up? Put a spring in your step? Although I don't want you off your game when you take my nephew back to your boudoir later.'

'I didn't know you had a boudoir,' Brian said.

'His ignorance knows no bounds,' Jackson said, pouring a small glass of sherry for Rita. 'Fiona is away doing some furniture shopping,' he explained, sweeping his arm around the room.

'This is some nice stuff,' Rita said, taking a sip.

'It's utter pish and belongs to a staging company who will be around forthwith to extricate it from the premises unless they want to come round tomorrow when they can fit the ashes into a bin liner.'

Rita chugged the sherry back. 'Aren't you having one?'

'As I said to one of my employees yesterday, it wasn't Butlins I spent my time in. We didn't have beer pong competitions to see who could get it up the jacksy first. Sobriety has been my old friend these past twenty-five years. Although I may imbibe at a later date, but today, alas, I have to watch the performance from the galleries.'

'What job is it you have for us, Adrian? The suspense is killing me.'

'I want us to go for a drive. And I'll show you.'

'Can I drive your new Jag?' Brian said.

'Can you fuck. Rita is going to have that pleasure. A big step up from that roller skate she drives. Now, let's go. We don't have all day.'

TWENTY-ONE

'You lot took your bloody time,' Paddy Gibb said from the doorway of the semi-detached house.

'What kind of Christmas spirit is that?' Andy Watt said.

'Bah humbug. Get your arse inside.'

'Maggie Parks not here, then? She always makes your cheeks rosy.'

Gibb ignored him as the three detectives followed Gibb into the house. They went through to a large room.

Jake Dagger and Kate Murphy were looking over the body of a man on a chair, with a bullet wound in his forehead and one in his chest.

'Edward Hopkins, aged sixty-seven, and all-round bad bastard,' Gibb said.

'You know him then, sir?' Hazel Carter said.

'No, I just made that up, Hazel.' He shrugged his hands into his pockets. 'Sorry. Yes, I know him. He came up through the ranks with the likes of Malky Mellon but the last I heard, he was working for Peter Stanton. Of course, he's a legit accountant, but he has connections to him.'

'Maybe not Mellon so much, nowadays,' Miller said.

'You don't need an accountant to see how many ciggies you have left,' Watt said. Then he nodded at the dead man. 'Any idea how long, doc?'

'I would say he was killed between midnight and seven this morning,' Kate volunteered.

'Who found him?' Miller asked.

'His cleaner. An old woman who comes in on a Saturday,' Gibb said.

'Sorry I'm late!' they heard a woman say behind them. DI Maggie Parks and her forensic crew. 'I had a busy night last night.'

'I'm sure you did,' Watt said. 'Round at old Paddy's again?'

'For God's sake, sergeant, please have a little bit of respect.' She smiled at Gibb who winked at her.

'Either shot could have been the fatal one?' Hazel asked Kate.

'Looks like it. But there doesn't seem to be any sign of forced entry.'

'That's my job to tell them that,' Maggie said. She looked at Gibb. 'There doesn't seem to be any sign of forced entry.'

'I was just saying to DI Miller that it could be that Hopkins knew his killer,' Watt said.

'Who came round to visit after midnight,' Miller said, 'according to the time of death.'

'Maybe it was an escort.'

'Does he look like he was fit enough?' Gibb said.

'He obviously has money, so maybe he paid for a girl's company.'

'He *is* wearing clothes and not nightclothes,' Miller said.

'Well, he answered the door to somebody,' Gibb said. 'Get uniforms canvassing. I saw there are a few trees in his back garden, blocking the view from the tenements on Mayfield Terrace, but somebody might have seen something.'

'I'll get onto it,' Watt said. 'Come on Hazel, let's make ourselves useful.'

'Stop fucking fiddling with stuff,' Adrian Jackson said from the front passenger seat, as Brian sat in the back and played with the window switch. 'You're letting the cold air in.'

'This is a nice car.'

'And I want it to stay that way. Keep your filthy mitts off the buttons.'

'How come you're just out of prison and you can afford a nice motor like this?'

'Mind your own fucking beeswax.' He turned to look at his nephew. 'I might have been banged up, but Fiona was running the show while I was away.'

He relaxed as Rita drove the car like an expert. 'Turn left here, into Bright's Crescent,' he said, pointing. She took the big luxury car from Mayfield Road into the side street. 'Second on the right. Glenorchy Terrace.'

'There's a police car up ahead, blocking the street. The one you want to turn into.'

'Keep driving. Slow down though so we can maybe see what's happening.'

'I could open the window and ask that copper,' Brian said.

'Or we could go back to your place and I'll put a belt round your neck and they could think it was death by auto-eroticism gone wrong.'

Rita slowed the big car and they all looked down the street to where the emergency vehicles were. It looked like something serious had happened.

'No doubt about it, that's certainly a fly in the ointment. I wanted to have a word with him, but it can wait. But I do have a Plan B.' He turned to look at Brian again. 'It always pays to have a Plan B.'

'So what is it, then? This famous *Plan B*?'

'Don't sulk like a wee laddie who just lost his ball. I have important work for you, Brian, and I have to know you're up to the job. You're the only one who I can trust, so let me know if you still want to earn some big ones. Then we can go to McDonalds for lunch. Get you a Happy Meal.'

Brian smiled. Rita shook her head and Jackson gave her a look. *Two people taking their daft laddie out for a drive.*

'He's the reason old people shouldn't fuck,' Jackson said.

TWENTY-TWO

'This is a smashing place you have here, hen,' Lou Purcell said to Amanda Cameron.

'I'm just the manager. I don't own the place.'

The restaurant was busy, brunch being a weekend special. The prices attracted a fair number of customers.

'Every ship has a captain, and you're at the helm of this place.' He washed his sausage down with coffee.

'Mind if I join you?' Amanda said.

'Pull up a pew.'

She sat down opposite him. 'Did Percy send you here, Lou?'

'What do you mean?'

'I mean, you were here last night, and now you're here today. Are you here to watch what Bruce is up to?'

Lou could feel his cheeks going red. 'Oh God, no.

You're right about one thing though; I *do* want to see Bruce. I'm just sitting here wondering how to go about it.'

'You want to see him? Can I ask you what it's about?'

'I don't mind if you're there when I talk to him, but he might want me to speak to him in private. Do you think he would be up to seeing me?'

'Oh, I don't think he would mind.'

'I don't know if he's up to being around the public again.'

'He is, trust me. He's over there gabbing to one of the customers.'

Lou turned round. The restaurant was tacked on to the back of the pub and looked like a huge conservatory. He turned round and saw Hagan. The ex-detective looked over and came across when he saw his wife sitting with a customer.

'Lou, isn't it?' he said when he walked over. 'Percy's dad.'

'That's right, son.' Lou was about to stand up when Hagan put a hand on his shoulder.

'Don't get up on my account. What brings you up here? Percy not trust me or something?' He was smiling when he said it but there was an edge in his voice.

'Grab a seat, Bruce. And no, Percy doesn't know

I'm here. I came up here all by myself. I'm a big boy now.'

Hagan sat down at the table, opposite his wife. 'I'm all ears, my friend.'

'I was going to ask for your advice, in a professional capacity.'

'As a former psychiatric patient?'

'A copper.'

'What about your own son? Percy has a lot more experience than I have.'

'I love my son to bits, don't get me wrong, but sometimes I think he was switched at birth. We like to have a laugh, but this little project I have going, well, he'd think it was a hoot and it isn't funny to me. I need to ask somebody's advice.'

'If I can be of any help, fire away.'

Lou pushed his plate away and wiped his mouth. 'I'm trying to search for my family. I found out I was adopted and I'm not sure what to do now. I spoke to the adoption agency, but they can only do so much.'

'What do you want to know?'

'I found out that my father was a judge, and that I had half-brothers. Two of them. I mean, they might be pushing up daisies now, but I would like to know. Maybe even write to them and see if they want to meet up.'

'That could be fraught with danger,' Amanda said.

'Or at the very least, it could come as a shock to them and they might not be too happy about having a sibling that their father… well, fathered.'

'I know. But I'm curious to know. What if they liked the idea of having a brother? Maybe if they had their own kids, they would like the idea of having an uncle. I just want to find out one way or the other.'

'I can help you with that. Let me make some calls and we'll get together.'

'I appreciate that, Bruce. I know you're busy with the pub.'

Hagan waved Lou away. 'I'm just biding my time until I figure out what to do with my life now.'

'I'll give you a call, eh? And please don't tell Percy about this.'

'Mum's the word.'

Competing banks had had major offices in George Street in Edinburgh, back in the day when the height of technology was getting your passbook stamped when you made a withdrawal. With the advent of the internet, bricks and mortar were being sold off in favour of online banking.

Some of the huge piles in the New Town were worth a fortune and were quickly snapped up by property developers. They were turned into bars, nightclubs, and boutique hotels.

'What the hell is a boutique hotel,' Fiona Jackson said to herself as she stood outside *The Pinnacle Hotel*, on the block between Castle Street and Charlotte Square. She stepped inside and walked up to the front desk.

'Can I help you?' the young woman asked. Fiona wondered if she knew what her boss was like.

'I'd like to speak to Peter Stanton.'

'Do you have an appointment?'

'No.'

'I'm not sure if he's here.'

Which was code for *I'll get rid of the bitch. Meantime, get security here.*

'Check. Make a phone call. He'll want to speak to me here, rather than me go to his home.'

The girl picked up a phone and called a number. 'Who shall I say is here?' she said before the other end was picked up.

Before it could be answered, a burly security guard approached her. 'Follow me,' he said.

'My husband knows I'm here,' she said to the man, 'just so you know.'

'Good for him. Does Santa know you're here too?'

'I hope you'll still have your sense of humour when I'm finished.'

The guard walked away and Fiona followed. Through to a back office that might have once been the seat of power for the bank manager, but which was now the seat of power for a shady businessman.

The guard showed her in.

'Mrs Jackson! To what do I owe the pleasure?' Peter Stanton indicated that she should take a seat.

'I'll stand. I won't be long. I'm just here to collect the cheque.'

'Oh. You collecting for charity or something?'

'That's not the sort of attitude that will keep your kneecaps from being detached.'

Stanton lost his smile. 'Just like you took care of the men that came round every month for some protection money? The last time I saw, they were both still standing.'

'That's because Adrian let them. Now, the cheque. Here's the amount you owe us.' She took a piece of paper out of her pocket and put it on his desk.

'I don't believe I have my cheque book handy.' He smiled again.

'Maybe you should ask your accountant to get you the money. Oh wait; he won't be able to do that anymore. God rest his soul.'

The smile vanished again. 'What do you mean?'

Now Fiona was smiling. 'Haven't you heard? Poor Edward popped his clogs in the early hours of this morning. Poor old sod. I heard it on the news. The police are treating it as murder.'

Stanton stood up so fast that Fiona thought he was going to leap over the desk at her, but she stood her ground. She'd had enough of his performances to last a lifetime. If he killed her right here, then so be it.

'If I find out you had him topped to try and put the frighteners on me, I'll—'

'You'll what?'

'You'll fucking find out.'

'Get the money, Stanton. Every fucking penny, or you'll pay, one way or another.'

'Get out. While you can still walk.'

'You have seven days. Or interest starts to get added.' She walked out of his office, knowing in her heart, that this would be *her* office one day.

TWENTY-THREE

Miller was in his kitchen making lunch. There was more snow forecast and he was starting to think they should up sticks and go live in Florida.

'You'll wear the bottom out of that pan,' Kim said, coming into the kitchen and putting her arms around him.

'Hey, I know how to cook.'

'You know how to open a can of soup and heat it up.'

'That counts.' He kissed her and poured the soup into two bowls.

'What was the shout this morning?' she asked him as they sat at the kitchen table.

'An accountant was murdered. Shot in the head and the heart.'

'A hit?'

'Looks like it. Paddy was talking to some of the undercover boys, and they have a file on him. Edward Hopkins. Gangland accountant.'

'Who was he working for?'

'We're still figuring that out, but early indications say he's working for Peter Stanton.'

'Stanton's been quiet recently, hasn't he?'

'His name hasn't been connected with anything, but he's always on our radar. He gets other men to do his dirty work.'

They ate their soup. 'Do you think Molloy is involved in this?'

Miller made a face. 'Nah, I think Molloy would have made the old boy disappear.'

'Unless he was sending a message to somebody.'

'It's a possibility, Kim, but I don't think that's Molloy's style.'

'Are you going to talk to him about it?'

'Not unless we have a definite connection. Besides, he's like a caged tiger right now. One of the guests at that crime-writing thing they've got going on has disappeared. There's some talk that she went off to find a man.'

'She's going to feel foolish if she comes back and finds out that the police are looking for her.'

'They seem like a bunch of yahoos that would panic at anything. Molloy will be pissed off if he finds out it's a publicity stunt, and she might disappear for real.'

They chatted for a little while. Miller was on the fence about whether to tell Kim he had been speaking to Venus. If he didn't and she found out, she would be angry with him. If he did, she would be angry with him. Better to get it over with.

'Venus was there,' he said, feeling like a man standing on the edge of a cliff.

'Figures. She works there, doesn't she?' Miller nodded. 'Yes, she does. She lives up in Lauriston now. She sold her place in Fife.'

'That'll make it easier to see her.'

'Easier for who? Certainly not me. I hope you're not thinking that I'll be popping in for tea and crumpets any time soon.'

'Not the tea, anyway.'

'Come on, Kim. We have a beautiful new daughter, a beautiful little girl, and you think I'm going to throw it all away on some woman I don't even know.'

'A woman who looks like your dead wife. Almost exactly like your dead wife. Her twin sister. It would be like you talking with Carol again.'

Miller knew his wife was having a hard time with Venus, but sometimes, things in life couldn't be changed. It wasn't as if he had invited her into his life.

'It just so happens that she works at the hotel, and

there's a missing woman. There's nothing I can do about it.'

'You could have somebody else deal with it.'

'Samantha asked me.'

'Oh well, if Samantha asked you, then that's okay.'

'Christ, Kim, I don't want a fight.'

She sighed and drank some coffee. 'Neither do I.'

He reached over and squeezed her hand. 'We're an even bigger family unit now. Carol was part of my life but that's my past. Venus is just here, that's all. Somebody I'm interacting with because of a missing woman. Nothing more.'

She smiled at him. 'I think things will be better when I go back to work. I know that's a way off, but I can't wait, to be honest.'

'And I'll do everything I can to support that. Just remember one thing; I love you, Kim Smith. It's you and I as a team now.'

'It's Kim Miller now. I'm not going to let you forget.'

Miller's phone rang. 'What now?' he said as he looked at the caller's name. 'Percy,' he said to Kim, getting up from the table.

'Sorry to disturb you again, Frank, but can you come down to the mortuary?'

'Sure. What's up?'

'I'll tell you when you get here.'

Miller drove his Audi A6 down to the mortuary car park, glad of the all-wheel-drive. It wasn't as good as a Range Rover, but it was good.

He stepped out into the cold, running his conversation with Kim through his head again. He was sure she had meant what he said, but there was a tinge of anger hovering about there. He had spoken to Venus, yes, but that was it. He hadn't tried anything on or said anything inappropriate. And he, Miller, was okay with Eric Smith, Kim's ex, speaking with her. Of course, they had to as they had a child together, but now so did he and Kim.

Christ, why did life have to be so complicated?

He walked across the slippery car park and was let in the back entrance by Gus Weaver, one of the mortuary assistants.

'It's a bit chilly for June,' Weaver said, grinning.

'We complain when it's too hot in the summer and too cold in the winter. We're a nation of moaners, Gus.'

'That's a fact.'

'Ah, mister detective. You are here again. You no want to stay away from me, yes?' Sticks was a young Polish female who worked alongside Weaver as an assistant.

'I'm spoken for, Sticks, but I hear Gus is available.'

She laughed and wagged her finger. 'Matchmaking with old man. Not so funny.'

'Hey, I'm right here,' Weaver said.

'No offense.'

'Offense taken. Old indeed. I bet Kim doesn't speak to you that way.'

'No, she doesn't. She knows better.' He made a slapping gesture with his hand as if he regularly smacked Kim's backside.

'I'll tell her what you're like in here, mind,' Weaver said. 'Slapping her arse indeed. She'd smack the shit out of you any day.'

Miller looked at Sticks. 'It's true. But take me to your esteemed leader.'

He followed Weaver through to the lift that would take them to the post-mortem suite upstairs. 'Got any plans for Christmas, Gus?'

'Is that an invite over to your place for dinner?'

'Did you hear the words *invite* or *dinner*?'

'There was an implication that an invite would be forthcoming.'

'You should try and read people a bit better. As much as I'd like to invite you...'

'No you wouldn't.'

Miller looked at him and grinned. 'You're right. Sorry, pal, you're stuck with... well, whatever poor sod is stuck with you on Christmas day.'

'You're a heartless man, Frank Miller. Don't you worry that I might be lying face down in the snow somewhere.'

'Oh, okay.'

The lift doors slid open and they walked inside the suite.

Jake Dagger, Kate Murphy, and Percy Purcell were all dressed in mortuary clothes with disposable aprons on.

'Get togged up,' Purcell said. 'We just found your missing writer. And she didn't die of natural causes.'

TWENTY-FOUR

Kim was putting the baby back down when the doorbell rang. 'Have you forgotten your key or something, Frank?' she said out loud as she walked down the hall.

She opened the door.

'Congratulations, Kim,' Venus Molloy said. She was holding a small bunch of flowers and a teddy bear.

'Oh. Thanks.'

'Can I come in? See the precious little one?'

'She's just gone back down to sleep.'

'I'll be quiet.'

What don't you understand? Do you think I said that so you can start a debate? 'No. I don't want to risk waking her up.'

Venus smiled and nodded but held out the flowers anyway. 'A peace offering. Can we talk? I promise I'll be quiet.'

Kim stepped aside and Venus walked into the hall.

'The living room is on the left. Go through.'

Venus handed Kim the gifts then took her coat off. Kim hung it up in the hall but when she went back to the living room, Venus had gone through to the kitchen.

'This is a nice place you have here,' Venus said, looking out of the window. 'Different from your house in Circus Lane. A lot busier here, isn't it?'

'We like it. Can I get you a coffee?'

'Thanks. Milk only.'

Kim put the kettle on and turned to look at Venus. 'You wanted to talk.'

'Look, I'm sorry you're upset about Frank seeing me, but we're going to run into each other now and again. I know I made a fool of myself earlier this year, but I didn't know how Frank would react to me being back.'

'I didn't say I was upset about Frank seeing you.'

'Oh. That's what he said. We sit and have a coffee when he's round at the hotel. He lets me ask him all about Carol in her younger days. I met her but I wish I could have spent more time with her.'

'I just don't want Frank going backwards, that's all.'

'What do you mean?'

'It took a long time for him to get over Carol, and

you coming into the picture has made him think about her again. I just don't want him upset.'

'That's not my intention. I just wanted to come up here to reassure you that I wouldn't want to come between you and Frank. I can make sure that if he comes into the hotel, that somebody else deals with him. The last thing I want to do is come between a man and his wife. You have to believe that.'

The kettle clicked off and Kim poured the coffees.

She sat down with the cups. 'Look, I appreciate what you're doing, but—'

Venus held up a hand. 'I work in the hotel so if I'm out and about and I see you, I don't want either of us to feel awkward.' She sipped the coffee. 'I want to assure you there is nothing between Frank and me.'

'I'm not saying that I think there *is* anything going on.'

'I apologise for the trouble I've caused between you and Frank.'

'That's certainly put my mind at ease, Venus.'

The other woman smiled and they made small talk while they finished their coffees.

As she put her coat back on, Venus once again reassured Kim that they could all live in peace.

As Kim closed the door, there was one small thing that niggled at her, but she couldn't put her finger on it.

She gently leaned her head against the back of the

door and closed her eyes. She disliked Venus Molloy more than ever now. She didn't trust her, and she certainly didn't like her.

'Fucking bitch,' she said softly as she walked back into the apartment.

They looked down on Amber Summers. Her pale, naked body lay on the steel table, like she was sleeping. Except for the hole in her face where her left eye had once been.

'Christ, how long did you say she was sat there?' Miller said.

'Over six hours at least,' Jake dagger said.

Miller shook his head. The complete disregard for human life amazed him sometimes.

'Even if somebody had bothered to check on her hours earlier, there was nothing they could do. The pen had been rammed right through her eyeball,' Kate said.

'And she was just sitting there, in the middle of the square? Nobody thought to go over and see if she was okay? That's a disgrace.'

'Lady Stair's Close opens up into a wide square, Frank,' Purcell said. 'Sometimes jakeys go there to sit and drink. This woman just happened to be sitting by the lamppost in the middle of the square. And whoever murdered her, staged it with a beer bottle, so she would look like another homeless person with a drink problem. And she was facing away from where the foot traffic would walk through from the High Street to The Mound.'

'Until somebody eventually found her and called it in,' Dagger said. 'After they saw her covered in snow and they thought she needed help.'

'But for the grace of God, eh?' Miller said. He felt angry and he didn't know why. *Don't you, Frank? Aren't you pissed off at your wife for not giving you the benefit of the doubt?*

'What time are we looking at?' he said.

'It's a little harder to tell, but we're thinking between eleven last night and seven this morning.'

'How in God's name did he get her to go there and then manage to kill her?' Purcell said.

'The Writers Museum is there. In the close,' Miller said.

They all looked at him.

'I don't think the location was random. She was a writer, had a pen rammed through her eyeball. Lee Foley was an editor and had a pen rammed into his ear, killing him. Maybe somebody lured Ms Summers there, or followed her. Those writers said they were heading out to do their own thing. We need to talk to them again.'

'Agreed,' Purcell said. 'Let's get this post-mortem over with first.'

'Did I tell you my old man found out he's adopted?' Purcell said, as they cleaned off and took their protective gear off.

'No, you didn't.'

'He found papers that my grandparents left behind, and in them, there's a letter from Grandma telling Lou that he was adopted.'

'Jesus. Imagine finding that out after all these years. How's he taking it?'

'He's fine with it. It's like a big adventure for him. Apparently, his biological father was a judge. Thomas Young. This judge was married with kids and Lou's mother was a maid in the house and the judge had his end away with her and got her up the spout. Then the maid had to go and give the baby up for adoption.'

'It must have come as a shock for Lou.'

'It was at first, but he's happy now that he's found out he has siblings somewhere. He wants to find them,' Purcell said, making a face.

'Really? Isn't that fraught with danger? I mean,

what if they get pissed off that their father was having it away with a member of the staff?'

'That's what I told him, but he won't listen. I also told him not to introduce them to me.'

'That means you might have nephews and nieces as well as aunts and uncles,' Miller said, smiling.

'Didn't you just hear me? I said I couldn't be less interested. Just because *daddy was a judge*, doesn't mean to say they're all there. They might be daft. Just look at Lou.'

Miller laughed. 'You're a bad bastard sometimes, Percy.'

'Aye, but I have the looks to go with it.'

'You shouldn't be quite so modest.'

'Come on, let's go and talk to those writers. See where they were last night and if they can prove it.'

They walked out to the car. 'How is Lou going to find out about his other family?'

'He'll just have to do a search. See if they really exist.'

As they got into the car, a sudden chill swept through Miller. And it wasn't the weather that was causing it.

TWENTY-FIVE

'I'm sorry to tell you all that Ms Summers was found dead this morning,' Miller said to the small ensemble. They were sitting in one of the conference rooms. One of the larger rooms with a small stage was to be used for the panels and discussions, but this smaller one was being used to announce the death of Amber Summers to the writing committee.

'My God, what happened?' Anthony Robson said. He was sitting in one of the chairs near the front, next to Paul Britain, who was in his wheelchair.

'She was murdered. And left in Lady Stair's Close where she was found this morning.'

'Jesus. Who would want to murder Amber?' Paul said.

'That's what we're trying to find out, Mr Britain.

We also want to know where each of you was last night.'

Robson smiled and leaned in closer to Paul Britain. 'I say, this is one hell of a crime writing convention. It's almost real.'

'I think it is real, Tony.'

'What? No. This is bloody good fun.'

'Each of you will be interviewed again.'

'Are you going to interview the guests who are part of the convention?' Paul asked.

'We're going to interview everybody. We'll have a team of detectives here shortly. Nobody is to leave the hotel. Now if you'll kindly stay here, we'll get that sorted.'

As Miller closed the door, Robert Molloy strode across to him.

'What the fuck are those mutants up to?' he said, barely containing his anger.

'I don't think they're up to anything.'

'This is some fucking stunt.'

'A stunt? Two people are dead.'

Molloy shook his head. 'I want them all out of here. Cancel that stupid writing thing they've got going on.'

'That's not going to happen. We want them all under one roof where we can keep an eye on them. At least until the seminar is over.'

Molloy turned and stormed off.

Venus had been talking to Purcell in the lobby but excused herself and came over to Miller. 'I was talking with Kim earlier.'

'Really? Where abouts?'

'In your flat. I took a new teddy up for Annie. Kim and I sat and had a coffee and now everything is good between us.'

'Well, I'm glad.'

'As long as she realises that you knew Carol long before you met *her*, Frank. Your past life is your past. However jealous Kim is, she can't take that away from you.'

Miller was lost for words for a moment. 'I'm sure she'll be fine. Her hormones have been all over the place recently.'

'I understand. I don't know if Kim and I will be best friends, but at least we can stop avoiding each other.'

'Detective Miller?' Purcell called.

'Excuse me, Venus.' Frank walked over to the superintendent.

'You looked like you could with being rescued,' Purcell said in a low voice.

They walked a short distance away, out of earshot of the other guests. 'I don't know what it is, but ever since Venus has started working for her father, there seems to be a new side to her.'

'In what way?'

'I don't know. She seems more confident.'

'Wouldn't you feel confident if your father was Robert Molloy?' Purcell glanced over at her.

'It's not that. She seems like a different person from the one I met a few months ago. Like there's an undercurrent. And she said she went up to the flat to talk to Kim.'

'Christ, I would have liked to be a fly on the wall there.'

'God, I'm going to hear about it later. Kim hates her.'

'Just hold on tight, and scream if you want to go faster. Isn't that what the sign says on the waltzers?'

'With the waltzers, it only lasts for three minutes.'

'Then you get off and puke your load. Just like being married, son.' Purcell shook his head. 'Right, let's get those interviews started when Steffi Walker and Julie Stott get here. I think Watt and Gibb are still tied up with the killing of the old boy. Bloody Christmas time. It drives everybody mental.'

'Tell me about it.'

'Are you free for a pint tonight?'

'What? Your wife kicking you into touch already? Don't you normally take Suzy out on a Saturday night?'

'Not every Saturday night. Sometimes we stay in and I show her a good time.'

'You mean you put the *Grease* DVD on?'

'Exactly. Chinese takeout, a bottle of wine and a bit of *You're the one that I want.*'

'The simple things in life. But I'm sure Kim won't mind me going out on the lash when she's been stuck in all day with the baby. Tell you what, why don't I see if Samantha can take the wee yins and bring Kim along. You bring Suzy.'

'That sounds good. But it's more of a business drink, Frank. Jeni Bridge will be there.'

Miller looked at his boss. 'What's going on?'

'I would rather her tell you. Say to Kim that Jeni is in a bit of a pickle and she needs our help. That will make things easier.'

'I hope so. I have enough trouble with Venus Molloy without adding to it.'

'All will be explained. Then it will either work out, or you and I will be living together.'

'Don't say that too loud, for God's sake.'

'I'm bored,' Brian said.

'I told you to get him a Happy Meal,' Adrian

Jackson said to Rita. 'The toy would have kept him amused for hours.'

'I thought there was going to be some action,' Brian said, his finger on the window switch again.

'Touch that fucking window button again and you'll be getting a bus home.'

'I could have been at the match this afternoon.'

'And going home to that filthy sewer you call home.'

'You get bored easily,' Rita said, pulling into the side of the road. The blue Transit van was parked outside the pub in Howe Street, an arterial road that led from George Street down to Stockbridge.

Skinny Malinky's.

'For fuck's sake, we'll get that changed for a kick off,' Jackson said, stepping out of the car. He leaned his head back in. 'Be a doll, and park round the corner. I'll call you when I need you to come pick us up. Brian, shift your arse.'

Jackson acknowledged the driver of the van. They walked up the steps into the pub which was crowded with Saturday afternoon drinkers. Jackson had his bowler hat on and held on tightly to his cane.

He walked up to the bar. 'Get me the manager,' he said to the girl behind the bar.

'Who are you?' she said, giving him a dirty look.

'Now.'

Sensing there might be trouble, the woman walked away.

'Did she just call me a wanker?' Jackson asked, turning to his nephew.

'I think it was prick.'

'You sure? I thought it was *wanker* myself.'

Nobody gave them a second look as Jackson brought his mobile phone out and made a call.

A few minutes later, a man appeared and approached.

'I was told you'd be coming here. I'll cut to the chase; get the fuck out of my pub, or I'll have big Simon over there rip your arms out of their sockets.'

'Let me make this easy for you, son. *You* get the fuck out of *my* pub.'

The manager laughed. 'You're a fucking joke, old man.' He turned to the bouncer who was sitting near the back, keeping an eye open for trouble. 'Throw this dirtbag out of here.'

Just then, the door came crashing open and twelve men walked in. They began ordering the punters to leave, assisting those who resisted.

The leader of the group walked right up to big Simon who was standing close to Jackson and, after Jackson pointed him out, the lead man headbutted him. Another man walked up and kicked the young man hard in the guts.

'What were you saying, fuck face?' Jackson said to the now-speechless manager. 'Get this place cleared and then we'll get this prick through to the office. He looked at the female bartender. 'And it's *wanker, sir* to you.'

'Oh. I didn't realise. I'm sorry. I'll get my coat.'

'Indeed you will not. How do you fancy being my new manager?'

'What? I don't understand. I insulted you.'

Jackson laughed. 'Trust me, I've been called worse. And nobody has the balls to talk to me like that and get away with it. I like your mettle. Even though you didn't know who I was, you still stood up to me. You're hired. Whatever he was being paid, I'll double it.'

'Sure. Thanks.'

Jackson led her by the elbow, skirting the last of the customers who were being extricated. 'I expect loyalty. In return, I'll look after you. Fuck me over, and I promise you'll live to regret it.'

'Trust me, I've worked for that pig for months and all he tries to do is grab my arse.'

'I promise you one thing, I will never grab your arse. I have a wife who would kill us both.'

'It will be a pleasure to work for a gentleman. But there's just one thing.'

'What's that?'

'I don't know your name.'

Jackson laughed. 'Adrian Jackson. You can call me Mr Jackson. That young man is my nephew, Brian. He's been coming round the places with me. He's my assistant.' He looked at the dozen men now standing around, having thrown Simon out. The leader was holding the manager. 'Those men work for me.'

'I'm glad to be on board, Mr Jackson,' the young woman said.

'And now you can tell me *your* name.'

'Sky.'

'Well, Sky, show me where the back office is. Then keep an eye on the bar.'

They marched the manager through to the back and he was roughly pushed in. 'Now, this is how it's going to go down; my lawyer has already drawn up the papers.'

'This place isn't for sale.'

'That's right, son, and it wasn't for fucking sale when your boss threatened my wife and made her sign it over. Now I'm back in town, and I'm going to take back what's rightfully mine. Including this pub. And every other place your thieving bastard of a boss stole from me. You understand?'

'Go fuck yourself. I'm not signing anything.'

'I know you're not, dimwit. You're just the messenger.'

Three of the men held the manager's hand down

while a fourth battered it with a hammer. The manager screamed. The man battered it until it resembled a hamburger, then took a towel and wrapped it.

'Tell Stanton, if he wants a fucking war, he fired the first salvo, a long time ago. And if he wants to stay and fight now, this is just the beginning. You got that?'

The manager nodded and held onto the blood-soaked towel. Then Jackson drew the sword out of his cane and ran it across the man's face. The manager screamed again.

'Now every time you look in the mirror, you'll remember what you said to this old man.' Jackson looked at his men. 'Get this piece of shite out of here. Drop him off at my new hotel in George Street. Tell Stanton I'll be calling by later. And to get his fucking stuff out of there.'

The men hauled the manager out. A few minutes later, there was a knock at the door. It was Sky.

'You still want me as the manager?'

'Double what he was earning. That offer still stands. If you think you can handle the heat.'

'I was brought up in Niddrie. It's only getting warm in here.'

He smiled at her. 'Good. Now, I have to leave. There will be men in here with you. Let's get this placed organised. We'll do a refit. Have a grand re-opening. And change that stupid fucking name.'

TWENTY-SIX

'We could get a babysitter. Go and have a drink,' Kim said.

'I have to meet Percy tonight,' Miller said.

'Percy? Really?'

Miller was sitting on his couch and sat forward. 'Yes, really.'

'Your female friend was round here this afternoon.'

'Who?'

'I think you know who.'

'Venus?'

'Funny that's the first name that should jump into your mind.'

'Being a detective, I deduced it was her. If it had been Hazel or any other female on my team, you would have used her name. And you know I don't have any female friends, so the logical conclusion was the woman you deem to be my friend.'

'It must hurt being such a smartarse.'

Miller stood up. 'Kim, honey, I love you more than you know. Venus isn't a friend of mine. And why was she round here?'

'Dropping off flowers and a teddy for Annie.'

'To be honest, when I was at the hotel earlier, she asked me if it was okay, and I told her I'd run it by you first. I see she couldn't wait for me to ask you.'

'I don't like the bitch, Frank. I don't like the fact that she knows things about me and I don't know one thing about her.'

'Like what kind of things?'

'Oh, this is a nice flat but not quite as nice as your house in Royal Circus,' she said in a mocking tone. 'Condescending cow.'

'I don't know why she would say that.'

'I don't want you telling her anything about me again.'

'I didn't tell her anything about you.'

'Nothing slipped into the conversation when you were having a wee chat about Carol?'

'I didn't tell her anything, okay?'

Miller racked his brain, trying to think of when he could have told Venus about where they lived. Or where Kim had lived before moving in here. Did his mind wander that much that he said something without realising it?

'She certainly knows, and *I* didn't tell her.'

'Maybe she was bringing the flowers as a peace offering.'

'Don't! Don't you fucking dare defend her actions. Did you tell her it was okay to come round here?'

'No, I didn't.' *So what if I fucking did?* he wanted to say but kept it in check.

'We've had this conversation before; you have to let go eventually.'

'For God's sake. I didn't invite this woman back into my life.'

'Just make sure she doesn't come round here again. I was only polite to her because the kids were in.'

Miller grabbed his coat. 'Don't wait up.'

'I'm sure Venus will have a nice bottle of champagne waiting for you,' Kim said, but Miller had already closed the front door.

He went downstairs and crossed the road. Logie Baird's bar in the hotel was busy. The heat enveloped him as he went through the doors, stamping his feet to get the snow off his boots. He saw Purcell standing up from a table and waving at him. As he got closer, he saw Jeni Bridge sitting at a table.

Purcell made a drinking motion with his hand; *want a pint?* Miller gave him the thumbs up and sat down at the table after taking his coat off and hanging it on the back of the chair.

'Snow at Christmas, who would have thought?' Jeni said.

'Hello, ma'am. At least the kids like it.'

'It's Jeni, tonight, Frank.'

Purcell came back with two pints and went back for the glass of G&T. 'Cheers,' he said, as Miller took his first sip.

'How are things with the new baby?' Jeni asked.

'She's got a good pair of lungs on her, that's for sure. And so has the wife, but that's another story.'

'Everything okay with Kim?' Purcell asked.

'Oh yes. Venus Molloy is the problem. She went to my flat with a gift this afternoon, and Kim can't help feeling jealous.'

'Take this from a woman's point of view, Frank; this is not a good situation. Kim has given birth to your child, she needs to feel loved and wanted right now, not thinking that her husband is seeing another woman behind her back.'

'I have no interest in Venus.'

'Kim doesn't know that.'

'I've told her often enough.'

'You have to *show* her. Make her feel special, that she's the only woman in the world who matters right now. Because, trust me on this, her emotions will be like a roller coaster and you don't want one of the cars derailing.'

'I wish to God Venus didn't work so close.'

'She does, so you'll just have to deal with it. I believe that you're on the case with the murdered writer?'

'I am.'

'You think one of them is the killer?' Purcell said.

'I think so. It's too much of a coincidence.'

'Agreed,' Jeni said.

Miller took a sip of his pint, feeling that if he started chugging it back, he'd be well blootered by closing.

'You'll be wondering why we asked you here tonight, Frank,' Purcell said.

'I thought it might be my initiation into your little club.'

'Trust me, we don't invite hooligans like you into the club,' Jeni said.

'It's a little more serious than that. Something that's going to need your full confidentiality,' Purcell said.

'Fire away.'

'I'm trusting you on this, Frank,' Jeni said.

'I appreciate that. Percy and I go way back.'

Jeni took a sip of her G&T. 'I know why Lee Foley had my name in his notebook.'

Miller looked her in the eyes, like he would look at

an interrogation subject. Took a sip of his pint before placing it on the table. *Don't tell me she fucking killed him and wants us to help cover it up. Please, God.*

'He was blackmailing me.' She took a sip of her own drink. Somebody brushed past Miller and he wondered for a moment if the man had heard Jeni's words, but if he had, he didn't look round.

'Why?'

'I dabble in writing and I sent some stuff to Foley for a cheap edit, so I could see an example of his work. I sent him my book when it was finished but I didn't hear from him again. For a while. So I wrote to him and he said the work was going to take a lot longer than he thought, so he wanted more money. Double what he quoted me.

'I told him I wasn't going to pay it. He said he wouldn't send me the book back, nor return my money, if I didn't pay him more. I refused and told him I was a police officer. I demanded my money back.'

'I'm assuming he didn't give it to you?'

'No. We had reached a stalemate, and he had the upper hand as he already had my money. I thought that was the end of it.' Miller liked the head of Edinburgh Division and he had never seen her like this. Usually, she was a strong woman who didn't shy away from anything, but now, she looked like a little girl.

'He didn't let it go, I assume,' Miller said.

'No. In fact, just when I thought it was quiet, boom, he blew me out of the water.' She looked at Miller now, like she was on the fence about trusting him. 'I need you to keep this between us, Frank. I trust Percy, would trust him with my life.'

'Just the fact he invited me along here tonight speaks volumes. He and I trust each other, Jeni.'

She took another sip of her drink, steeling her nerves. 'He sent me a letter with a pack of photos. Apparently, he had come up to Scotland to talk to me in person, and unfortunately for me, he chose the very weekend that a friend of mine stayed over.'

'Nothing wrong with that.'

'There were photos of us kissing in the living room. Taken through the window. Like a fool, I didn't shut the curtains.'

'Christ, he's the one who was spying on you. How can he blackmail you for that?'

Jeni looked at Purcell who nodded.

'The friend who stayed over was my ex-husband, who is the Chief Constable of Police Scotland.'

Miller took a drink. 'Is your ex in a relationship?'

'Yes. He's married. My daughter is away through to Glasgow to spend Christmas with them. Happy families.'

'And he stayed over at your place and now Lee

Foley was blackmailing you because your ex spent the night.'

'Yes. I swear I just kissed him. It was his birthday. We'd been out for his birthday. My daughter wanted him to come through and celebrate as he'd already celebrated with his new wife, so he came through and we had a drink and he slept in the spare room. My daughter was in the house for God's sake. But Foley didn't know that, or didn't care. I gave Alistair a kiss for his birthday, big deal.'

'That's the thing,' Purcell said, 'even though Jeni didn't do anything, just the photo of her kissing her ex would be on the front page.'

'He'd have to resign. We both would. The scandalmongers would make sure of it, but it would also ruin his marriage.'

'You paid Foley the money.'

'Yes, I did.'

'And let me guess; he came back for more.'

Jeni sipped more of her drink and her cheeks were getting redder as her anger started to come out. 'Not only that, but he told me he was coming up to Edinburgh to see me and a few other,' finger quotes, '*special clients*. Other writers he was no doubt blackmailing.'

'That list he had in his notebook was probably the list of people.'

'And they're all here at that writing conference,' Purcell said.

Miller finished his pint. 'Which means the murderer is right there, under our noses.'

'Somebody wanted to put a stop to Foley,' Purcell said. 'But why kill Amber Summers as well?'

'And is he going to stop at those two?' Jeni finished her drink.

'I think the murderer is going to kill somebody else,' Miller said. The other two officers looked at him, waiting for him to go on.

He shrugged. 'It's simple; one was killed by ramming a pen into her eye. The other by a pen rammed into his ear. See no evil, hear no evil. And now we're just waiting to find out who won't be able to speak no evil.'

TWENTY-SEVEN

'I thought you wanted one of those big, army-looking things?' Larry said, peeking out of the kitchen window at Scramble's new purchase.

'Fuck that. This Discovery has heated seats *and* a heated windscreen, so I won't have to spray de-icer all over it and freeze my nuts off while it's defrosting.'

'It looks a smart motor. Going to let me drive it tonight?'

'Am I fuck. Your big arse will bend the leather seat out of shape. Besides, we should take that heap you bought today. It's got the petrol cans in it.'

'This van is anonymous. They'll think you're a rich farmer when they see you driving that thing.'

'Don't talk pish.' Scramble looked at his watch. 'We better get going. It's late enough now.'

'One o'clock in the wee hours of Sunday morning? The town will be jumping right now.'

'They'll be too pished to notice us.'

'Let's hope so.' Larry pulled on the old work boots he had bought at a charity shop. Which would be wiped clean and dumped in a street bin. 'You ready?'

'I was born ready.'

Larry shook his head. 'Watching too many movies again.'

They went out the kitchen door. Larry had traded in the small car for a white Transit van earlier that day, while Scramble had been out buying his used Land Rover Discovery. Now the van was running, with the petrol cans in the back.'

'What a piece of shite, compared to that thing,' Scramble said from the passenger side. 'I'm surprised you can even squeeze in behind the steering wheel.'

'Nobody looks twice at a white van. They're two a penny. Plus, where we're going, there's work being done, so it won't look out of place. If we get stopped, then we say we've got cans of petrol for the generators.'

'Aren't generators diesel?'

'Fucked if I know. Some daft copper won't know the difference. As far as he's concerned, we're going to a building site to drop off some shite for Monday morning. Besides, they're too busy on a Saturday night. They'll be fighting some drunks round about now.'

The snow had stopped falling earlier, and he had already wiped the snow off the front of the van. He was careful when he drove out, but the road was deserted. It also meant it wasn't ploughed or gritted, so he kept the speed down.

The back end slid out a few times but he managed to get it up to the main road without putting it through a hedge.

'Ravelston, eh? Bet some snobs live there.'

'Ours is not to judge, Scramble my old friend. Ours is to burn and kill. Although we've been assured the place will be empty.' He turned to his friend in the dark. 'Our contact did say it was going to be empty, right?'

'Yep. More's the pity. It's been a long time since I've set some bastard on fire. That was a right laugh.'

'We would have been fucked if we got caught.'

Scramble laughed. 'It's the thrill that keeps us going.'

'It's the money that keeps me going.'

'That as well.' Scramble looked at the map. The van was a basic vehicle, with no frills. He took a little torch out and began tracing the route.

'I'll stick to the main roads. We should be okay that way.'

'Fine by me. I don't want my arse going through the windscreen.'

Larry headed down to Corstorphine and along one of the main corridors going into Edinburgh from the west side. There were a few cars going about but most of them were taxis. A night bus heading out of town. The road was pretty well ploughed.

It wasn't much further along the road to Murrayfield, which was another upscale enclave, butting onto Ravelston. He turned into Murrayfield Road and carefully drove to the top of the road and turned left into Ravelston Dykes Road.

'The house used to belong to a judge, apparently,' Scramble said. 'I Googled it.'

'And now it belongs to our target and we're going to turn it into a pile of ashes.'

Scramble smiled at the thought. 'Easy number, if you ask me. Money for old rope, as me old dad used to say.'

The road veered round to the right, and the entrance road to the house was on the left. It was shared as an access road for the golf club, used by maintenance vehicles. The back end of the van slipped sideways but Larry corrected it and drove along the road.

The house was on the right. The whole place was being done over. Stripped out and everything new put in. There was scaffolding on the outside of the house and the front driveway and garden resembled a building site, which it was.

A couple of skips sat in the darkness, building material covered in snow, and planks of wood sticking up in the dark as the van's headlights picked out the debris.

'I'll back it up to the door and if it's locked, we'll jimmy it.'

Larry backed it up and stopped. 'In and out, five minutes,' he said, killing the headlights.

The circular driveway was pitch black. They took flashlights out of their pockets. Small ones so they could see. Scramble put his under his chin and made a face.

'For God's sake. It's an improvement, I'll give you that, but we're not here to piss about.' He opened the back doors of the van and they grabbed a large can of petrol each. Walked up to the front door, careful not to slip on the untreated pathway.

'What about our footsteps in the snow?' Scramble said.

'They're not going to think the place torched itself, and we bought old boots from a charity shop. We went over this. We take them off when we get back in the van, put them in a bag and dump them.'

'I know. I'm just saying.'

'Put it into fucking gear, for God's sake. When this stuff goes up, it's going to go like Guy Fawkes night.'

The front door was locked, but Larry brought out a

small crowbar and went to work. Then it was open. They took the petrol cans inside then went back for the other two.

'Take yours through the back and I'll do the front. When yours are lit, get back through here and then we'll light mine.'

Scramble nodded and disappeared with the cans. Larry heard them being kicked over then a whoosh as the petrol was lit.

Scramble came running through to the front where Larry was. 'Right, get going, sunshine,' he shouted.

The inside had cans of paint and wood lying about. No furniture but the house would go up quickly. Larry kicked over his own cans and when the liquid was out and spreading about, he lit a piece of newspaper and then chucked it onto the petrol.

It took hold immediately and they could see the back of the house as it was lit from the fire. The flames danced around in the darkness for a moment then quickly lit up the whole room.

'Let's get the fuck out of here.' Larry made for the door and Scramble didn't need to be told twice.

Two minutes later, they were in the van and driving away.

'I hope you boys have some nice stuff in here,' the postie said to himself, shining his torch around the driveway. Larry was the big guy, and he didn't know what the smaller one's name was. The mail always came for Larry Cresswell, and despite him trying to strike up a conversation, the smaller one was always guarded.

They must have a lot of valuable stuff in there. This house must be worth a few bob, he thought, shining his torch over the Land Rover Discovery that was parked outside. Maybe they had friends over, or they had splashed out on a new car.

Must be nice.

He himself drove an old Vauxhall Astra that was second-hand. He couldn't afford a nice new car like this.

'Buying a new car, and I'll bet they won't even give me a tin of shortbread. Well, fuck 'em. I'll just help myself to whatever pressie I want.'

He shone the torch into the kitchen window. He wondered if they could fight. The big fella looked like he might put up a fight, but maybe he was the wife in the relationship and couldn't fight through a wet hanky. He'd known blokes like that.

Round the back, the kitchen door was locked. Everything was locked. What the fuck was wrong with people nowadays? Didn't anybody trust anybody?

What happened to the good old days when you went out and left your front door open? This wasn't Wester Hailes after all. There wasn't much chance of coming home to find your junkie neighbour hooring into your best bottle of Scotch in this neighbourhood.

The only junkie you would find was one who had travelled here and was now tanning your house.

'Like I'm doing,' he said, chuckling to himself. This would be the third Christmas in a row he'd picked on a tight bastard and nobody was any the wiser. A lot of people blamed the refugees who were living in Edinburgh now, but that was just stupid. He was more worried about his next-door neighbour who had lived here all his life than he was of some poor sod looking for a safe place to live.

Some people were fucked in the head, that's all.

He had his gloves on of course, and not just because it was cold. A backpack too, for his loot. He was making footprints in the snow, but there were already footprints here and tyre tracks where another vehicle had driven out. Quite a big one, by the size of the tracks. A van maybe. Although he hadn't seen a van round here recently. Doesn't mean to say they hadn't gone out and got one.

They must be making good money, whatever it was they did. This house alone must have cost them a few quid. He'd only been on this run since last March and they were here already, and he didn't know how long they'd lived here.

The kitchen window was locked too. He went back to the door and took out the bump key he'd bought online. He'd practised using it on his own front door. He put the key in and gently pulled on the handle then hit the key, bumping the tumblers inside.

The handle turned, and the door was open. He took the key out of the lock and quietly walked into the kitchen. Stood and listened for the sound of somebody waking up from a deep sleep, but heard nothing.

He walked through to the living room. A Christmas tree was up but there were no gifts underneath it. No worries; the whole house was filled with gifts for him.

If you don't think of your postie at Christmas, then he's going to think of you. And chorey all your stuff. That was his motto.

He saw an iPad sitting on a table. He lifted it and took off his backpack and put the device inside. A watch on the sideboard. *Citizen.* He shrugged. Beggars couldn't be choosers after all, and it was one of those *powered by light* jobbies, so he slipped it into his pocket.

He'd long ago given up the idea of taking DVD players and stuff like that. Every man and his dog had a DVD player, so it was the laptops and things like that he wanted. He knew a dodgy little geezer in the pub who could move it along, for a cut of course.

He shone the light around the room but didn't see any more electronics, apart from the big screen TV, but it's not the sort of thing he was interested in lugging along the road to his car.

He went into the hall, careful where he put his weight. The tyre tracks meant they could have gone out on a hooly, but it could equally mean they had entertained visitors who were now gone. He wondered if they had separate rooms.

The first door was a bedroom. He went inside, glad to see that there was nobody sleeping in it. And there it was, the MacBook Pro, sitting on a little desk, the green light on the charging end of the cable telling him to go ahead and chorey it.

He followed the wire to the plug and pulled it out of the wall. The green light died and then it and the computer went into the backpack. A quick scout of the room and nothing else jumped out.

The next room also contained an empty bed, but there was a Kindle sitting on the bedside table. At least one of them wasn't an ignoramus.

The Kindle went into his bag. The torch swept around the room. Nothing else worth nicking here that he could see. A quick squint through some of the drawers, but he didn't do what other housebreakers did;

ransack the place. No, it was always better if they didn't know they had been burgled until much later. The first reaction would be, *Has anybody seen my iPad?* Daft bastards.

He sniggered to himself in the dark as he made his way back to the kitchen. He didn't want to be too greedy, so he decided to call it a night.

'I bet you won't have half as good a haul in your sack as I do, Santa,' he said, laughing.

'Is that right?' a voice said from the dark.

The postie stopped in his tracks, his whole body tightening. He could make out a figure in the dark off to one side. There was nothing he could say, was there? He was in here when he wasn't supposed to be.

The frying pan smacked him in the face, breaking his nose. Hard, but not hard enough to knock him flat.

He expected the lights to come on, but they didn't. That meant only one thing; they didn't want to draw attention to themselves.

'I'm sorry. Please let me go,' he stammered, blood now leaking from his nose.

'Oh, I don't think so, Santa. You've been creeping about here, poking your nose in where it wasn't wanted. And now you have the audacity to break in. Luckily for us, we have covert cameras that sends us a warning on our phones.'

That's why I didn't hear you drive up. You parked

close by and walked, didn't you? He wanted to ask but thought better of it. Better to stick to begging.

'Please, just let me go. You can have your stuff back. I'll request a different route. You'll never see me again.' He took the backpack off and put it on the floor.

'You're right about that; we won't ever see you again,' Scramble said and fired the first shot into the postie's heart. Larry opened the cellar door and held the man at the top of the stairs. He quickly let go and stepped to one side as Scramble fired another shot into the man's head.

The postie fell backwards, dead before he hit the bottom of the stairs.

'First class,' Scramble said. 'Get it? First class.'

'Oh God. Don't give up your day job.'

TWENTY-EIGHT

'I want that bastard taken care of,' Peter Stanton said, pacing about in front of the living room windows. His girlfriend, Chrissie Green, put two cups of coffee down on the dining table.

'We're working on it, my love.' She stood looking at him, at the walkers cutting across The Meadows, walking dogs in the snow.

'The fucking audacity of the man! Going into one of my pubs and kicking everybody out. And having old Hopkins topped!'

'Not exactly your pub, Peter. Legally, I mean.'

'You know what I mean. Nobody would have been any the wiser if he had stayed in prison.'

'Well, he didn't, so we'll have to deal with it.'

Stanton paced around the room. 'What's next

though, Chrissie? That wife of his walks into George Street and demands money. Just like that.'

'Money you took from them.'

'Whose side are you on?'

Chrissie sat down at the coffee table and sipped at her coffee. 'Sit down and drink your coffee and I'll ignore that last remark.'

Stanton took a deep breath and stomped over, sitting down opposite her. 'Sorry. I'm wired up.'

'I can tell. That's why I made yours decaf.'

'It's not funny.'

'I'm not laughing, Peter. I'm keeping a cool head. Unlike you. We have a problem and we have to deal with it.'

'Did you hear the news this morning?' Stanton ran a hand through his hair.

'No. I was in bed.'

'There was a fire last night. A house was burnt to the ground. Arson, they're saying. And you know whose house it was?'

'No.'

'Michael Molloy's. Michael fucking Molloy. Somebody is going to have his kneecaps taken off. And by *somebody*, I mean Adrian Jackson.'

'Michael Molloy has a lot of enemies. He should learn to keep his emotions in check. It wasn't necessarily Jackson who was responsible. I'm sure Molloy has enemies lined up waiting to have a kick at him.'

'But still. They'll be looking at Jackson. The police.'

'Jackson is certainly causing trouble for himself. I never thought he would be quite as bad as this.'

'I have to go.'

'Where?'

'To make sure the hotel in George Street hasn't burned down.'

'She'll be fine, as long as she's well wrapped up. The fresh air will do her good.'

'It's cold,' Miller said, watching as Kim put Annie in a little suit. 'She's too little.'

'Stop fussing like an old hen,' Kim snapped. 'Is it because you're hungover?'

'I'm not hungover. I had a few beers, that's all.'

'You were banging about when you came in. I'm surprised you didn't have to do a commando crawl just to get into bed.'

'For God's sake, now you're just exaggerating.'

'I am not. Your breath stank.'

'Just get the baby ready and we can go for a drive. I'm going to have to go to work today.'

'Really now? And where would work be? Don't tell me; at that fucking hotel. With Miss Prissy Pants. Why don't you just move in with her? You see more of her than you do of me! And the cheek of the woman. Coming round here and pretending nothing's wrong.'

'Nothing *is* wrong.'

'Yes, there is. She's in our lives and I don't want her in my life.'

'I'm meeting Percy in a little while.'

'Why didn't you say that? I wouldn't have bothered getting our daughter dressed.' Kim lifted the baby and went into their bedroom, closing the door behind her.

Miller shook his head. He got himself into trouble just by doing nothing. He would be glad when this investigation was over. But he would have to go to the hotel and tell Venus Molloy that they wanted the guests to stay another night.

Because one of them was a killer.

He left the apartment and walked along to the lifts where he bumped into Samantha Willis.

'Hey, Frank. What's wrong, sweetie? You feeling tired?'

'Hi, Sam. I am a bit tired, but it's not that. Kim's annoyed that I've had to be in contact with Venus Molloy. I can't help it; she's involved in this investigation.'

They stepped in after the doors opened. 'I heard

about Amber Summers. First that editor, and now her. It's a stressful time. Especially for the lady who's just given birth to another human being.'

'I know. Maybe she'd like a girl's night out soon.'

'I'll organise it. Kate Murphy, Hazel Carter. Anybody else who would like to come along.'

'Steffi Walker and Julie Stott are always up for a laugh.'

'Leave it to me, Frank.'

'Thanks, Sam.' The lift doors opened. 'How's Jack this morning?'

'Your father is up and at 'em. He's meeting with some of his friends today.'

'Lucky him.' Miller pulled up his collar as they stepped out onto the North Bridge, the snowing starting to fall again.

They parted ways and Miller walked down the pavement, his boots crunching the snow. No matter what way he looked at it, he couldn't see a way that Kim would be happy.

He stepped up to the hotel and walked into hell.

What was supposed to be a cosy meeting of writers had turned into a rabble. People were shouting and screaming, and Miller half expected chairs to be flying.

The group of writers who had paid to come to Edinburgh to see the all-stars of the self-publishing world were sitting watching the so-called big names having a slanging match.

Venus Molloy was trying to calm them down. 'If you'll all just give me a minute, I'm sure we can sort this out,' she said, but the voices continued.

'Shut up!' Miller yelled. The voices stopped. 'This lady is trying to help you, so we need you all to be quiet. I'm sure you all love the sound of your own voice, but we need you to be quiet now.'

He stood and waited, his face flushed with anger. He couldn't shout at Kim, but he could certainly shout at these cretins.

'What's all the fuss about, anyway?' he asked when everybody calmed down.

'My wife's missing!' Paul Britain said. He was agitated, moving his wheelchair back and forth in a slight motion, like an able-bodied person might do if they were standing on their feet.

'Come with me,' Miller said. Turning to Venus he asked, 'Can we have a room again, please?'

'Of course.'

She led the way and Anthony Robson pushed Paul in his chair. They went into a small conference room.

'I'll get some coffee, Frank. You look like you could use it.'

'Thanks.' His anger was still raging through his

veins now, which made him think that if Kim saw him with Venus now, he couldn't care less.

'Tell me about your wife, Mr Britain, and why you think she's missing.' He felt like he was experiencing déjà vu.

'She was here last night. We were in the bar. Constance wanted to speak with some of the writers, as the evening event was basically an informal get-together in the bar. She was happy, even though it was marred by Amber's murder.' Paul let his head fall onto his chest and he sobbed for a moment.

Just then, Andy Watt knocked on the door and walked in. 'I just got the call, boss. Got here as soon as I could.'

'We have another missing person,' Miller said, and Paul looked up at the other detective.

'My wife's not in her room. She didn't come back last night.'

Watt looked at him. 'You have separate rooms?'

'Yes. In case you hadn't noticed, my legs are round and attached to a chair.'

'And that means your wife can't sleep in the same room with you?' Miller looked at him.

'Being disabled doesn't mean you have to sleep in the same bed, does it?' Robson said.

'It works for us,' Paul said. 'When we go on holiday, or away for an event like this, it's just the same as at home.'

Watt shrugged. *It takes all sorts.* 'Tell us more about last night. When was the last time you saw your wife?'

'She was with me,' Robson said.

'Sit down on one of the chairs,' Miller said, and he thought Watt was about to add, *You're making the place look uncomfortable,* but he didn't. Robson sat down, next to Paul.

'You were the last one to see her?' Watt said.

Miller was taking notes.

'I don't know if I was the last one, but I was certainly with her in the bar. We were discussing a collaboration. I was excited about it, to be honest. A new series. We were plotting and planning. Constance is a brilliant writer and for her to take me on board is just fantastic. She likes my work she said.'

'She does. She likes his stuff,' Paul said. 'She and Tony would be a dream team.'

'You were sitting in the bar and...?' Watt said.

'Then one of the writing group came across and interrupted us, but it wasn't as if we could complain. That was what the evening was all about.'

'Who spoke to you?'

'I'm not sure. A man with a beard, but I could have sworn he wasn't part of the writing group. He seemed to know her though, but that's not surprising since she's a bestselling author.'

'Anybody else see this man?'

'You would have to ask them.'

'She's going to be found dead, isn't she?' Paul Britain said, his eyes red from crying.

'We don't know that, Mr Britain,' Miller said, without much conviction.

The door opened again and Paddy Gibb walked in. Miller saw Steffi Walker and Julie Stott standing behind him.

'A word, inspector,' Gibb said. Miller got up and joined the DCI in the hallway.

'We ran a background check on those writers. Nothing. Not even a parking ticket. None of them are in debt, apart from the usual bills, and none of them have ever been arrested. We're working through the attendees. So far, zilch.'

Miller wanted to tell Gibb about Jeni Bridge being blackmailed, and that maybe somebody else was being blackmailed, but it wouldn't do any good. The blackmailer was dead, so why kill Amber Summers?

'Do you think maybe this Britain woman killed the editor and the Summers woman?' Gibb asked.

'She's a person of interest, certainly, until we find her and can question her. I did find an address book in her room. We could look through it and see if anything jumps out.'

'Unless we find her dead,' Steffi Walker said.

'The thing is, we don't know where she could have gone. She's a visitor in the city,' Julie said.

'I'm leaving these two with Watt,' Gibb said, turning to them. 'Try and stay out of trouble.'

'I'll keep an eye on them,' Miller said.

'No you won't. You're coming with me.'

'Where are we going?'

'Have you seen Michael Molloy or his father since you came in here?'

'No, why?'

'That's because they're somewhere else. And that's where we're going.'

TWENTY-NINE

Miller parked the pool car behind the fire engines. They couldn't get closer to Michael Molloy's house because of the fire hoses snaking everywhere.

'There's not much left of the house,' Gibb said as they got out of the car. 'Couldn't have happened to a nicer psycho.'

'Remember the judge who died here?' Miller said.

'How could I forget? Molloy got a bargain, I reckon. It's probably fucking haunted.'

'It's a nice place. Up a lane that's shared by the vehicles from the golf club. No next-door neighbours. A slice of the country, right here in the city.'

'Not far to go for Molloy to bury the bodies on the golf course.'

They walked towards the driveway and heard shouting. 'I don't fucking care! I have stuff in there!'

Michael Molloy was standing face to face with a firefighter, while his father was next to him, trying to calm him down.

When Robert Molloy saw Miller and Gibb, he strode across, his feet sinking into the snow that hadn't already been trampled.

'Have you seen this?' he said.

'Well, we've only just got here, Molloy, so that would be a no.'

'Don't get fucking flippant with me, Gibb.'

'Easy there, Molloy, or we might haul your arse in for questioning.'

'Have a fucking word with yourself.'

'*Jewish Lightning* I heard one of the firefighters say.'

'That's fucking slander. I don't need the insurance, Gibb,' Michael said, coming across to the two detectives. 'Although when I find out who did this, they better have good private medical cover.'

'The incident commander said it's a definite case of arson,' Miller said.

'No shit. I get a call this morning to say my house has been burnt down, so it wasn't me leaving a cigarette in the ashtray.'

'It was a nice place,' Gibb said. 'Maybe a jealous neighbour didn't want you turning a nice, old house into a modern interpretation of its once former glory.'

'I think we both know you should be talking to Adrian Jackson,' Robert said, his breath coming out like smoke. He was shivering inside his coat.

'Why would you say that?' Miller said.

'He's just back in town and Stanton's accountant gets murdered. Now Michael's house gets torched. It doesn't take Stephen Hawking to work that out.'

'Do you have any proof that Jackson was behind this?'

'Of course not. Otherwise, we wouldn't be standing here. We'd be busy arranging something else.'

'Where were you both last night?' Gibb said.

'I was at home,' Robert said.

'I was in the new hotel, where I'm staying, with my girlfriend. We got a call from your uniforms to get down here.'

'This is a disgrace,' Robert said. 'If that wee fanny is back home flexing his muscles, he chose the wrong family to fuck with.'

Miller looked at the house again, with smoke still coming out of it in parts. It was a blackened shell.

'The fire investigation team will be looking around the property, but it seems that a large amount of petrol was used on the bottom floor. Whoever it was, they didn't mess about and they knew what they were doing.'

'That hardly makes me feel better, Gibb,' Michael said.

'Just don't go doing anything stupid, son,' he said, knowing the warning would fall on deaf ears.

'Oh, I guarantee when I do something, it won't be stupid.'

'Hello!' Adrian Jackson said, opening his door wider. 'I was wondering when you would come round for tea and biscuits.'

Miller and Gibb stepped into the hallway of the expensive apartment.

'We came round to see how you're settling in,' Miller said as they walked along to the living room.

'No you didn't; you came here to see if I killed Edward Hopkins and torched Michael Molloy's place.' He indicated a settee. 'Please, sit down.'

'How did you know we were going to ask about that?' Gibb said.

'Both things have been in the news. Molloy's bonfire was on the radio this morning. So naturally, you came along here to see if I had ash on my shoes and petrol on my trousers.'

'We don't think you would dirty your own hands,' Gibb said.

Jackson sat down on a leather chair. One of his new ones. 'You can ask my beautiful wife where I was last night. Fiona, love?'

Fiona Jackson came through from the bedroom, her hair looking like it had been in a fight with a badger. And lost.

'What time is it?' she asked.

'Police time. Inspector Miller and DCI Gibb came round for tea and crumpets. Except we have no crumpets.'

'We don't have any tea either,' she said, reaching for a packet of cigarettes.

'Bit early for crumpet anyway,' Gibb said.

'Speak for yourself.' Jackson grinned while his wife made a face. 'Fee, could you do us some coffee, please love?'

Fiona ambled away with all the enthusiasm of somebody on death row.

'How have things been since you got back?' Miller said.

'It's been two days, inspector, and already I feel like the people of Edinburgh want to throw a parade.' He reached over to a side table and held out the letter for him to read.

The threatening letter.

'When did you get this?' Gibb asked after he read it.

'It was waiting for me when I arrived home. Obviously, some people in the community don't have the same bonhomie and community spirit that others do.'

'Could it have been any of your neighbours?' Miller asked.

'Could have been, but let's not be silly about this; the Robert Molloys of this world weren't exactly waiting with open arms.'

'Anything else?'

'Well, there hasn't been a horse's head left in the bed yet, if that's what you mean.'

'We can see about getting you police protection,' Gibb said.

Jackson laughed. 'Although your offer is very kind, a cousin of mine down in London has very kindly leant me some of his staff until I can hold a recruitment drive. Besides, how would that look to anybody driving by? Adrian Jackson needs his hand held.'

Fiona came back with the coffees and Jackson hoped she hadn't made the coffee with hot tap water again.

'We won't tolerate people thinking they can run about in this city doing whatever the hell they like,' Gibb said. 'You might not believe this, but the law-abiding citizens outnumber the scum.'

'What the chief inspector is trying to say is, if you

step out of line, we'll be all over you like a rash.' Miller stood up.

'I'm here to start a new life. A quiet life. Maybe people should stop poking their nose into my private life.'

'Just make sure your private life doesn't become a public one.'

THIRTY

'What are we going to do with this smelly bastard?' Scramble said, putting a hanky over his face. Larry shone the torch around the cellar. There was one little light hanging from the middle of the ceiling. This was a rental property, and they had no use for the cellar.

'We'll have to bury him.'

'Here?'

Larry tutted. 'It's a pity NASA doesn't recruit from Scotland. You'd be their catch of the day. Of course not here. In the woods somewhere.'

'I'm not putting him in my new Land Rover.'

'Nobody said anything about your precious new motor. We can put him in the van.'

'Thank fuck for that.' Scramble looked at the postie's corpse with disdain. 'I told you there was something about that prick.'

'We'll deal with him later. We have a busy day ahead of us.'

They walked up the stairs to the kitchen. They had cleaned it after killing the postie and they had no doubt that luminol would bring up the residue of blood if it were to be sprayed just now, but a little bleach later on would scrub it clean.

'I have to say, I'm bloody knackered,' Scramble said. 'Those bloody petrol cans were heavy.'

'I didn't think they were. But maybe to a short-arse like you.'

'Big, bad, Larry, eh?' Scramble shook his head. 'Get the frying pan on again, cock. I'm going to the phone box.'

'You want the works again?'

'Of course I do, Larry. Burning houses down gives me an appetite.'

'Well, nash then. This stuff won't take long to cook.'

'It won't take long in the four-wheel drive.'

'You and your bloody toys.'

'I won't be long. All we need is the schedule and we can make plans. And put some fucking clothes on. Going about in your vest and skids. I swear to Christ.' He shook his head.

'I'm roasting.'

'Don't be turning the fucking thermostat down again.'

He left the kitchen and Larry heard the car start up. A couple of minutes later, the big car was heading out of the driveway.

Larry let the frying pan heat up. He always liked to laze about on a Sunday, and today, he felt tired like Scramble. He thought about kicking this lot into touch, just go and live abroad and life would be less complicated.

He looked at the pile of mail still sitting on the kitchen table and wondered how long it would be before the postie was reported missing. He wondered if anybody had known he was coming here to rob. If they did, that might pose a problem.

If push came to shove, they would burn the house down and leave. Everything was in the fake names they sometimes used but getting new IDs wouldn't be a problem. They could even use the ones they had in their fire safe until they could get brand new ones.

He picked up the mail and went through it. *How many trees had to die to produce this junk mail, just for it to go straight into the bin?* He tossed it into two piles; crap and bills.

Then he saw the letter from his ex-wife again. He had given her his address in case of emergencies.

Despite what Scramble thought, Larry and his ex had split on good terms.

He ran his finger inside the seal and tore it open. Maybe she was toiling for Christmas money. He wouldn't be averse to sending her some. She had been good to him when he came out of the army, looking after him when he was going mental. Truth be told, that was why they had split up.

He read the letter. Scramble was wrong; Larry's ex didn't want to come to Edinburgh; she was already here.

He didn't hear the car coming back, but there was a knock on the door.

'For fuck's sake. Where's your key—' he started to say, but it wasn't Scramble standing on the doorstep. It was two men.

'Mr Cresswell? I'm DCI Gibb. This is DI Miller. Can we come in and have a word?'

THIRTY-ONE

The detectives stamped their feet before entering the house. There was the faint odour of cooked food, or something burning in the frying pan.

The big man was dressed in his underwear.

'If you give me a minute, I'll go and get my joggers on.' Larry Cresswell walked down a hallway and into a bedroom, closing the door behind him.

'Bit cold for going about in your pants,' Gibb said.

'It takes all sorts,' Miller said, looking around the living room. It was kept clean with only a copy of yesterday's *Caledonian* ruining the illusion.

There were no photos, nothing of a personal nature lying about.

A few minutes later, Larry came back into the room having put on sweat pants and a sweatshirt.

'Sorry about that. I don't usually have to worry

about going around in my skids.' He came into the living room and turned the gas fire on. 'Please, have a seat. Can I get you any coffee?'

'No, we're good,' Gibb said. They sat down on a settee.

'What can I do for you, detectives?'

'We'd like a word about Constance Britain. How did you know her?' Gibb said, stepping away from the fire.

'What about my ex?' Larry sat on a chair.

'Constance Britain, is your ex-wife?' Miller said, surprised.

'Yes. What's happened?'

'She's missing, I'm afraid,' Gibb said. 'We were wondering if you had heard from her?'

'Constance? Missing? How is she missing?'

'She's up here at some writing festival, and she was last seen last night, leaving the hotel with a man. She never returned to her room.'

'Good God. You don't think anything's happened to her, do you?'

'We're not sure yet. But another member of the group was found murdered.'

'Oh my God!'

'We're trying to establish who she spoke to, or who she was with. We found a note of this address in her room, which is why we're here. Have you spoken to her at all since she came up to Edinburgh?'

'No, not at all.'

'Do you keep in touch with her?' Gibb asked.

'Oh yes. We talk all the time. When we got divorced, it was amicable. Constance always had her head in a book. She very rarely wanted to go out anywhere, unless it was to an author signing.'

'Where are you from, originally?'

'Here. In Edinburgh. Constance is from Essex, but you wouldn't think it with her posh accent. It's fake, but she's not doing any harm. We lived down there, but I decided to come home after we got divorced.'

'Can I ask what you do for a living?' Miller said.

'I'm a freelance financial advisor. I also dabble in the stock market.'

'Oh, I see. I thought maybe you were a builder or something. I saw the white van round the back.'

'Oh, that? Nah. I'm just planning on doing this place up and it's easier to take the van along to the DIY store. Plus they're cheap to run and insure. I've never been into flashy cars.'

'Do you know if your ex-wife was depressed recently?' Gibb said.

'If she was, she didn't say anything to me. The last time she called, she told me she was putting on a little writing thing up here and I could go along if I wanted.

But to be honest, it's not my thing. I don't read crime novels.'

'Have you met her husband, Paul?'

'Paul? Who the hell is Paul?'

'Her husband. Paul Britain.'

Miller watched the big man closely, saw puzzlement hit his face.

'I've never heard of Paul Britain. She would have told me if she got divorced again and married somebody else. I've never heard her mention anybody called Paul. Britain is her writing name. As far as I knew, she was still married to Lee.'

Miller exchanged a look with Gibb before looking back at Larry. 'Lee who?' he asked.

'Lee Foley. The editor.'

THIRTY-TWO

'What in the name of Christ were the police doing here?' Scramble said, coming into the kitchen.

'Asking about my ex. She's missing apparently.'

'Just as well you sent me a text. I was on my way back. You didn't tell them about me, did you?'

'Of course I did. I also told them about the dead postie in the cellar.' Larry shook his head. 'No, they think it's just me who lives here.'

'The lease is in your name anyway, so they won't know I exist.'

'Unless they go talking to the neighbours.'

'You don't think they would do that, do you?' Scramble threw the newspaper down on the table.

'I don't see why they would. I mean, it's not as if Constance lives here. She's up from Essex with that fuckbag of a husband.'

'Somebody topped that bastard.'

'What? How do you know that?'

Scramble tapped the paper. 'It mentions it in today's paper. The police are still looking for the public's help in regard to the murder of Lee Foley, found dead in a rented apartment in Edinburgh.'

'Christ. What the hell has she got herself into?'

'It also mentions the murder of that other writer, Amber Summers.'

'She and Constance were friends. What the hell is going on?'

'Why don't you call her?'

'I just did. After those coppers left. There was no answer. No voicemail, nothing.'

'You got a letter from her, didn't you?'

'I just opened it when you went along to the phone box. It says she was coming up for that writing festival and if I wanted to get together, then to give her a call.'

'And you didn't call her?'

'No, Scramble, I didn't call her. I wish I had now. I'm not into all that artsy-fartsy stuff, but I could have met her for a drink.'

'What are you going to do now?'

'What can I do? I can just hope that she's away doing some research for her next book or something. But anyway, what did our handler say?'

'The client wants things ramped up. Every day. A

bonus will be paid if we can manage it since there are risks involved with such short-term planning.'

'Did you tell him we'd do it?'

'I said I would run it by you first.'

Larry nodded. 'Fuck it. Why not? I think we should get the hell out of Dodge afterwards. We can find a new base to operate out of.'

'Why all the hurry? Do you think the coppers will be back?'

'I don't think one of them will. His name is Frank Miller. And he's one of our targets.'

THIRTY-THREE

'They think because they're crime writers that we won't find out that there're shenanigans going on,' Gibb said, lighting up a cigarette. 'You don't mind, son, do you? The fucking things are killing me whether I'm smoking them or not. Either the lungs are fucked, or the head's fucked. I don't know which is worse.'

'You're the boss.'

'I am, aren't I? So shut your pie hole.' Gibb coughed up a lung and blew smoke out of the window which he had rolled down slightly.

'I think we need to speak to Paul Britain.'

'Why would he say Constance was his wife?' More sucking on the cigarette, more smoke blowing.

'Let's ask him.'

Gibb threw the spent cigarette out the window. 'What's your opinion of Jackson?'

'I don't think he shot Edward Hopkins. Unless his wife had things planned well in advance.'

'She managed to get the flat in Ravelston bought well in advance.'

'She sold properties they had and combined the money to buy that place. They have some boozers that are bringing in money, but so were the other flats they owned. Plus they've had their flats since before Jackson went inside so they made a good profit, even after the 2008 crash. What would his motive be to kill Hopkins?'

'He worked for Jackson many moons ago, before he jumped ship and went to work for Stanton.'

'Twenty-five years is a long time to harbour a grudge, Paddy. I can't see it myself. Molloy has been enemies with Peter Stanton for years, so maybe Molloy was behind it.'

'I wish we could put them all on a ship and sail them out to sea and cut them loose.'

Miller parked on the North Bridge outside the hotel and put the police sign in the windscreen.

The writers were found in the bar. Steffi Walker and Julie Stott were there, talking to guests. Venus was around. *As usual,* Miller thought. Life had been simpler when his fellow officers had been hunting him down as a felon.

'We need to speak to Paul Britain,' Miller said to her. 'Do you know where he is?'

'He went out with Tony Robson.'

'When?'

'Not so long ago, Frank. Ten, fifteen minutes, maybe.'

'You didn't happen to see which way they went?'

'No, but they left through the side door that has the wheelchair ramp.'

'Thanks.' Miller walked along the hallway, down some steps and past the reception area at the side entrance. Outside, he could see the wheelchair tracks going along the short esplanade to the North Bridge. He walked along, but there were crowds of people out doing Christmas shopping. The footsteps had churned up any signs of wheelchair tracks.

He turned and walked back into the hotel. Venus was talking with Gibb, so he made his apologies and took the DCI to one side. 'I haven't seen the crime scene photos from Lady Stair's Close, have you?'

'No, why?'

Miller stood thinking for a moment. 'They sent Maggie Parks and her team after it was discovered that Amber Summers was murdered. But she was found at the base of the decorative lamppost, which wasn't on the direct path as people came down the close and crossed over the square to go down the steps that lead to The Mound.'

'I know that. That's why she wasn't found until the morning. What's your point, Frank?'

Miller held up a finger. 'I need to call Maggie and have those photos sent over to my phone. I want to see something.'

He called Maggie and they spoke for a few moments.

'Is everything alright, Frank?' Venus said, coming back over.

'I just need to speak with Paul Britain. Can we look at his room? Tony Robson's too?'

'No, you won't be able to do that without a warrant. Sorry. It would be bad for business. I hope you understand.' She smiled and walked away.

They watched as Robert Molloy came over. 'That bloody house was starting to take shape,' he said.

'Why aren't you still down there?' Gibb said.

'Doing what? Standing around in the snow, freezing my nuts off? Even Michael gave up the ghost. He couldn't be parted from his girlfriend for too long. But why are you looking so glum? I should be the one who's upset, having a guest being murdered.'

'There's a couple of guys we want to talk to. We got some information that makes them look dodgy. I wanted to look in their rooms but we don't have a warrant. Yet. Venus told us about protocol.'

'Two dodgy bastards in my hotel, trying to make an arse of me? Fuck the warrants. I'll get the key and the manager can open the fucking rooms. If I find out some twat has been arsing about in here, by Christ, they won't be cashing in any of their frequent-flyer miles, I can assure you.'

'I'm assuming Constance Britain's room was checked, to make sure she hasn't come back?' Miller said.

'Yes, sir, it was checked earlier,' Steffi Walker said.

'Check it again. Just in case she's been back.'

Molloy turned round and strode off to the reception desk and spoke to one of the girls. A minute later, the manager came out of his office with a master key.

As Miller, Gibb and the other two detectives stepped into the lift, he saw Venus Molloy standing talking on the phone.

They got off on the third floor and walked along to Paul Britain's room. Steffi and Julie waited by the other room. The manager knocked and let them in. As expected, Britain wasn't there.

The two detectives looked around the place.

'Has the room been cleaned yet?' Molloy said.

'Housekeeping should be here shortly, sir.'

'It doesn't look like it's even been slept in,' Miller

said. There were no personal belongings in the room except for a suitcase sitting on a suitcase stand. The drawers were empty. The wardrobe was empty.

'I think he might have left,' Gibb said.

'His suitcase is still there, sir,' Miller said.

'Get it open, then.'

Miller pulled on latex gloves and lifted it on to the bed. Opened it. Inside was the printed copy of a novel. *The Beast Within* by Amber Summers.

'Get the other room open, son,' Gibb said to the manager.

They left Britain's room and went next door to Robson's. This room was in complete contrast to the other one. It looked like a teenage boy was staying here, with clothes strewn about the floor. The bed was unmade. Trash was on the floor, sweetie wrappers and plastic packets that sandwiches came in.

Miller noticed something. He picked up two shirts and looked at each of the labels. 'One is medium size, the other is extra-large.' He threw them back down on the bed.

'You thinking that maybe Robson and Britain are sharing a room, even though they have separate rooms?'

'That's the vibe I'm getting.'

'Dirty bastards,' Molloy said. 'What is this place, a fucking knocking shop?' He turned to the manager. 'Get some of the boys up here. Get their shite out of here. And make sure their fucking bill is made up and add on some charges for having their stuff packed. Make sure that's an extra that's listed.'

'This makes sense,' Miller said. 'Britain – or whatever his real name is – said that he and Constance have separate rooms. That's because they're not husband and wife.'

'If they're not married, what's their connection?' Gibb said.

'I have no idea.'

'I do,' Steffi Walker said, knocking on the room door. She was holding up a copy of a book written by Constance Britain. 'It has a bio page in the back. It says she is married to Paul, who she helps to look after. He's in a wheelchair after a skiing accident.'

'We know that Constance Britain was married to our murdered editor, Lee Foley, so why does that bio say different?' Gibb said.

Steffi held up the book. 'Anybody reading this would think she's a saint. That gets her the sympathy vote. Making it look like she's a good person.'

'She's next on the list. We need to find those two before they find her. Tony Robson and Paul Britain.'

Miller's phone dinged and he opened up the message. Downloaded the photos he'd requested. He showed them to Gibb. 'Wheelchair tracks in the snow near to where Amber Summers was found.'

'Where the hell would they have taken Constance Britain?'

'Speak no evil,' Miller said.

'What?'

'Foley was killed by having a pen shoved in his ear, Amber Summers by a pen in her eye, right? Hear no evil, See no evil. That leaves speak no evil. Didn't I see a flyer that Constance Britain was giving a talk tomorrow at the Bedlam Theatre? That's just up the road a bit.'

'Let's go.'

THIRTY-FOUR

It was a five-minute drive, up South Bridge, then Chambers Street and into Bristo Place. The two unmarked cars parked at the side and the four detectives poured out and walked through the snow to the main entrance of the theatre, which was once a church, built in 1840.

Now it was a small theatre, popular as a fringe site.

They'd called for backup. It was only a few minutes out.

Miller opened one of the front doors and they quietly stepped inside. They could hear raised voices.

'Is there a play going on?' Gibb said.

'Not that I know of.' They walked into the entrance foyer and opened the inner doors.

There, on the stage in front of them were Paul

Britain and Tony Robson. Britain wasn't in his wheelchair anymore.

The detectives walked forward as the two men stopped arguing. They both looked at Miller.

Britain looked wildly around him as if trying to decide which way to run.

'Don't bother. You won't even make it outside.'

The uniformed backup that had been requested arrived and Britain's shoulders slumped.

'Get down off the stage,' Gibb ordered, practically shouting.

'I don't think so,' Tony Robson said, pulling out a large knife.

Gibb backed off and made a gesture for the others to follow suit. 'Take it easy there, son. Come down and we can talk.'

Robson laughed.

'Where's Constance, Tony?' Miller said.

'Well, how the fuck would we know where the bitch is?' He was smiling like a maniac and waving the knife about. 'We came here to kill her. We thought she was here, poncing about on the stage where the *dahling* of the literary world will be strutting her stuff tomorrow night. But once again, she has to go and hide somewhere and pretend she was nearly a victim. She'll be a fucking victim alright when I catch up with her.'

'Where's your wheelchair, son?' Gibb asked Britain.

'It was a fake, dummy,' Robson said, answering for him and Miller knew Gibb would be seething inside, his Irish temper barely being held in check.

'Just tell us where Constance is,' Miller said. 'You don't have to hurt her.'

Robson gritted his teeth and screwed his face up. 'Am I talking Chinese? How fucking thick are you? I know all coppers are thick bastards, but didn't I just say we don't know?'

'We don't know,' Paul said. 'That's the truth.'

Miller looked at Gibb. *Are they telling the truth? What reason would they have to lie?* 'Come down and we can talk about it.'

'Go fuck yourself. Get out of here and mind your own business.'

'Not going to happen, Tony.' Miller took a step closer to the stage. 'Come on down. Put the knife away.'

Robson just looked at them all.

'Paul, why don't you tell us why you murdered Lee Foley?'

'Because he was a scumbag!' Robson shouted before Paul could answer. 'Blackmailing his estranged wife. Blackmailing us!' He used the knife to point between himself and Paul. 'And then he took up with that whore, Amber. And she was a million times worse than he was!' Robson's voice was raised now, spittle flying from his mouth.

'Is that why you killed Amber as well?'

'Well, duh. Of course it is. Foley edited Constance's books – very badly, as it turned out – and she didn't want him editing any more. But he had access to her files, her ideas, her plots. He shared them with Amber. She was going to be the next big one, even though she couldn't write a fucking grocery list.

'But Constance bounced back, and she wanted to get noticed. So me and him helped her, and in return, she would help us with our writing. She would back us, get us noticed. And it was all going fine until Amber stuck her nose in. Helping to blackmail us. Constance thought we could sort things out at this crime festival, but Queen Amber wanted to be number one, so she told us to our faces that she was going to destroy us. And she would too! She has a big following of readers, a bunch of illiterate bastards who think her books are fantastic when they're the biggest pile of shite I've ever read!'

'Did Constance know what you were doing?'

'No. She had nothing to do with this. It was all our idea.'

'No!' Paul shouted. 'It was all your idea! You said we would get away with it, that Amber would be out of the picture and we would make a lot of money! This was all you!'

'Either way, we would be rid of her and carry on as we were. Show some fucking gratitude, you whiny little bastard!'

'Come and speak to us, Tony,' Miller said, and later on, when he thought about what happened next, he would question himself over and over, whether he could have reached Paul Britain in time, whether he could have jumped up on the stage, and despite knowing that there was nothing he could have done, he would always doubt himself.

Tony Robson walked forward and Miller thought he was going to walk off the stage, now that he had said his piece.

Instead, he reached a hand round Paul's head and calmly slit his throat with the knife. As the blood shot out of the carotid artery, Robson let out a yell and pushed Paul off the stage.

Miller saw the man flying through the air at him but there was nothing he could do to stop the falling dead man.

As the life ebbed out of Britain, he crashed into Miller, knocking him to the floor, and all Miller could hear was men and women shouting and the thud of running footsteps.

Tony Robson calmly walked over to the centre of the stage, and it was if he was a magician. He simply disappeared into the floor.

As he landed on the padded mat below, he rolled off it and pulled it out of the way. The first uniform who jumped through shattered his leg in four places.

Then Tony Robson was gone.

There was chaos, with uniforms running up onto the stage as some grabbed hold of the still warm corpse of Paul Britain, who was lying on top of Miller. The corpse had headbutted the detective, a feat he couldn't have pulled off more perfectly if he had been alive.

Miller groaned as blood ran down his face.

'Steffi! With me!' Julie Stott shouted, and the two detectives ran out the front door of the theatre.

Julie turned right at a run, with Steffi hot on her heels. They were into Bristo Place, slipping on the snow on the pavement. A small alleyway ran from the theatre out to the street. The women had their batons drawn and Julie saw Robson as he ran along the alleyway.

'Stop! Police!' she shouted.

Robson turned to her and swung the knife, but the move was clumsy, and Julie smacked the knife away as Steffi moved in and brought her baton down on the arm, and again. Julie grabbed him by the hair and dragged him down onto the snow-covered pavement.

Robson dropped the knife as Steffi dropped on top of him, her knees digging into the killer's back.

'Anthony Robson, you're under arrest,' Julie said. 'This is over.'

THIRTY-FIVE

'I'm fucking knackered,' Scramble said, turning the heat up in the van as Larry started driving, the headlights bouncing off the fresh snow. 'That was heavy going last night.'

'Stop your whining. We have more to worry about than being knackered.'

'Like what?'

'Like the police coming round to our house. Like my Constance being reported missing. I wonder what she's got herself mixed up in now.'

'I thought she was minted, with all the books she sells?'

'She's worth a few bob, I'm sure, but that's not got anything to do with it. She wouldn't just disappear. I know her better than anybody. Better than that ponce she got hitched to.'

'And now he's dead.'

It doesn't surprise me that somebody topped him. I wish I'd done it. I always hated the little fucker. Made my skin crawl.'

'You met him?'

'I was at their wedding.'

'I wonder what went wrong with their marriage.'

'He was a weasel,' Larry said. He looked at the dashboard clock; 11.47 pm.

'You don't think we've taken on more than we can handle, do you?' Scramble looked worried.

'What? Naw, of course not. We're getting well paid for this gig, and in a few days, it will be over. Then we can start somewhere else.'

'A little change will do us good. Maybe we should go to the Canaries for a week. Live the high life, get us as many women as we can handle.'

Larry smiled in the darkness of the van. 'Sounds good to me.' He slowed the van down at the traffic lights. They were on Ferry Road at Goldenacre. Larry drove through and turned left into South Trinity Road then right into East Trinity Road and to their final destination, Russell Place.

'Jesus, they're nice gaffs round here. I mean, talk about private. Half the houses have ten-foot walls at the front.'

'To keep hooligans like us out.'

'It's going to take more than a ten-foot wall to keep this bad boy out.' Scramble laughed in the darkness of the van as Larry killed the engine.

'The house we want is back there. Ten-foot wall, but a twenty-five-foot driveway. Something like that. Either way, it's relatively long, which means the house is sheltered from the road.'

He had parked the van up, round the corner in the next street to the one they wanted. He'd thought at first that the van might stick out, but there was a joiner's van round the corner. Even here, white vans were accepted, if they were parked on the street.

'You ready, big man?' Scramble said.

'Indeed I am.' He took a bag out of the back which had plumber's tools in it. If anybody questioned them, they were emergency plumbers. They wore dark jackets with rolled up balaclavas on their heads.

They came to the driveway, which was almost like a country lane. Bushes and trees on either side. The driveway had snow on it, two tyre tracks from a car running the length of it.

They walked up. No security lights came on. No alarms rang out, although Larry would have been surprised if one did. On a property like this, it would be a silent alarm, and that would only go off if a door or windows were breached.

'Round here,' Larry whispered, pointing to the left.

They walked in the middle of the drive, knowing they had to be brazen about it. If a light came on and a door opened, they would give a fake name they were looking for, say they had the wrong house and leave.

No light came on, nobody shouting. The front door was here, with a parking area in front of it. There was a garage round the back of the house. They walked past the front door and slipped round to the right where there was a lush garden, enclosed by the high, stone wall. The garden carried on round the back and was bordered by the garage block.

Larry put the bag down and took out a crowbar.

'Keep a look out,' he whispered.

'This is not my first job,' Scramble said, looking around. 'Just hurry up with the fucking crowbar.'

Larry did his stuff, and soon the window was sliding up. They stood and waited for thirty seconds, knowing if an alarm was going to go off, now would be the time.

'You want to go in first?' Larry said.

'Since we don't know if there's a radge Dobermann in there, you can have the pleasure.'

'It would fucking spit you out. Then lick its arse to get the taste out of its mouth.' The window was higher off the ground, and Larry was struggling to get a grip on the wall with his boots.

'Give me a shove,' he said.

'For fuck's sake.'

'Hurry up.'

Scramble pushed Larry's backside, listening to the man grunt.

'You need to drop a few—' he started to say, but Larry was gone. Then his head popped up and looked out.

'I said, whoa, fucking numpty.'

'I thought you said, go. So I pushed harder.'

'Fuck's sake. Get a move on.' He reached his hand out, grabbed the offered bag and then pulled Scramble up and into the living room, not letting his friend's hand go until he had face-planted the carpet.

'I said fucking let go,' Scramble said as he got to his feet.

'Did you? I thought you said pull more.'

'Lying bastard.'

'Come on, we're making too much noise as it is. And shut that window before she hears anything.'

The house was a large detached number, with a guest suite tacked on to the side.

'And to think he bought this house with all his ill-gotten gains,' Scramble said as they checked to see the ground floor was empty.

They made their way upstairs. The intel they had been given said the room they were looking for was third on the right.

Larry stopped and nodded at Scramble, who nodded back. Then the men pulled the balaclavas down over their faces. Larry didn't believe in faffing about. He gripped the handle, turned it and stormed into the room. He dropped the bag and took the silenced gun from his inside pocket.

Scramble shone the torch on the woman's face just as she woke up and her eyes went wide, a split second before she could scream.

The bullet caught her in the forehead and as her body sagged backwards, Larry fired into her chest. Three times. He'd been told to make sure this one was dead before they left.

'Can't get any more dead than that, eh?' Scramble said and then he put his gun away, picked up the bag, and both men walked downstairs. There was one more instruction with this job.

Larry picked up the phone and dialled 999. When the operator answered on the other end, Larry counted to ten then hung up. They climbed out of the window they had come in. That was the instruction, and to leave it open behind them.

Six minutes, from the time they had climbed through the window to leaving.

By the time the first police car arrived, the white van was gone.

THIRTY-SIX

'Oh, I don't know about this,' Rita said from the driver's seat.

'What happened to the Jag?' Brian, in the back, opened the window again, down and up, down and up.

'This is less noticeable. And stop playing with the fucking switch. Did I not tell you that already with the Jag? Always fucking touching stuff,' Adrian Jackson said.

'It's a nice motor. Can I have it when we're done?'

'I tell you what you can have; my cane right up your fucking arse.' He looked at Rita. '*Can I have it when we're done.* You're getting a big enough bonus. Besides, this is Fiona's car. She'd rip your nuts off and give them to Rita for a pair of earrings.'

'Where are we going?' Rita said, guiding the little

Honda CR-V round the corner on the southern edge of Heriot's Rugby Club into Warriston Gardens.

'Straight on, love. It will become quite apparent any moment now.'

'You weren't having us on when you said we would be getting well paid, were you?' Brian said.

'No, I meant it. See those blokes that my cousin sent up from London? They'll look after us no problem until I can get men working for me, but this is a job that requires finesse.'

'Requires what?'

Jackson looked at Rita and shook his head. 'Six kids my sister had. Six. I wish to Christ she had bought a telly after the fifth.'

The car headed up the driveway leading into Warriston cemetery. Rita turned to look at him. 'Tell me this is a wind-up, Adrian.'

'Now just calm yourself down there, Rita. All will be explained when we get inside.'

The headlights picked out the gravestones, and with the snow on the ground, the cemetery wasn't as dark as it normally would have been.

Vehicle tracks had already been made in the snow; hearses and maybe workers vans. The little Honda made good progress along the track.

'Why are we going in here?'

'Have patience. You'll see in a minute.' He turned

to Rita. 'Follow the road round to the left. Then stop at the little mausoleum.'

'Oh, wait a fucking minute. This place is giving me the fucking shitters,' Brian said.

'There's a lady in the car. Watch your mouth.'

'You swear in front of her.'

'Never mind what I do, nob end.'

Brian made a face and looked out of the window. 'I don't like this at all.'

The car's headlights picked out the mausoleum which sat on the hilltop, at the side of the crypts. It looked like a small house, with red glass in the roof and was made of white marble, designed in a gothic style.

'Let me make this clear, son; I need your help. I'm in no physical condition to do this myself. Rita here is on board, that's why she's driving. And you don't hear her whining like a wee fanny, do you?'

'No.'

'You're a big, strapping young man. I need physical help. When we've done this job, you will have dosh in your pocket; more dosh than you ever dreamed of. You and Rita here can get a place together. She'll be able to catch up with the mortgage payments, that will take the pressure off from the bank then she can sell it.'

Rita turned her head sharply. 'Sell my home?'

'It makes sense, love. You'll get a good price for it

and you can invest some of the money and get a place with Brian.'

'My Malky won't like that.'

'Malky is the least of your worries. If push comes to shove and you work for me, somebody will have a word in Malky's ear. He won't bother you, that I can promise.'

Jackson remembered what Brian had said about seeing Rita as a bit of fun, but he thought the age difference might work for them.

'I need you now, son, and if you don't want to help, then we'll go back, I'll drop you off and you can go back to living in your hovel without two pennies to rub together.'

Brian sat silently for a moment, thinking through his options.

'We don't have all night, Brian. It's a simple yes or no.'

'Okay. Sorry I crapped out. I'll help you.'

'Good man. Rita, park at the side, there's a doll.'

She moved the car over to the side of the mausoleum. 'You know, some people might think those comments are sexist.' She looked at him. 'Calling me *love* and saying things like, *there's a doll.*'

'I'm just trying to be friendly, Rita. It's just how men my age talk. I know the world was knocked off its axis when I was put into prison, but I didn't think that men saying that would be seen as an insult. What say you, Brian?'

'I didn't say a word.'

'This is the twenty-first century,' Rita said. 'I might be some dumb blonde who fell for the charms of Malky Mellon, but I do have feelings, Mr Jackson. I don't want to be taken advantage of.'

'There, there, lo... I mean, sweetheart.'

'Now you're just taking the piss.'

Jackson laughed. 'I know, I have to adjust, so give me time.'

'Does that mean you won't slag me off either, Uncle Ade?'

'There we go with the fucking *Ade* thing again. I think you're just pulling my pisser, you wee toerag.' Jackson turned to look at him. Does that answer your question?'

'Adrian! Sorry, Uncle Ade, I forgot to call you Adrian!'

'I swear to God, why I haven't smacked the shit out of him by now, I don't know.' He opened his door and the car stayed in darkness. He had made sure to keep the interior lights off. 'Keep the engine running, keep all lights off and honk the fuck out of the horn if you see anybody coming. Oh, and don't be fucking smoking in the car.'

Brian got out the back as Rita switched the lights

off. Jackson stepped out into the cold and pulled his beany hat down tighter. It was the first time he'd been out without his bowler hat on.

The cold air hit them like a hammer. Jackson had two torches in his hands. He gave one to Brian and shone his own on the mausoleum.

'Get the bag out of the boot.'

Brian walked round to the back, lifted the tailgate and brought the black workman's bag out then closed the car up again.

'Very nice, but can we go now?' Brian said.

Jackson grinned. 'I like a man with a sense of humour.'

'I thought not.'

'Luckily for us, there are scallys going about who think nothing of coming into this sacred place after dark and fucking about with gravestones and the like. And some of them even venture into mausoleums, maybe to take shelter from the elements, maybe to smoke weed. Whatever it is, some filth has broken the lock on this place a long time ago.' He stepped forward and turned the metal handle. The ornate door with the red glass in it creaked open like in a cheap horror movie. He turned to look at his nephew.

'We're going in there?' Brian said.

'Come on, it's not haunted.'

'How do you know?'

'Well, if it is, we'll soon find out, won't we?' Jackson stepped inside the mausoleum, his feet crunching stones and dirt on the old, stone floor. At the far end was a sarcophagus with an elaborate stone carving sitting on top.

'The Stanton family did have high expectations for themselves. I mean, look at this. Who the hell do they think they are? Fucking royalty?'

Brian shone his torch around the interior, the light bouncing off the dirty marble. 'Why are we in here?'

'All will be revealed in a second.' Jackson swept parts of the floor with his boot and revealed two ring-pulls set into the concrete floor. 'Lift that one up and we'll pull at the same time.'

'You mean... we're going to lift the trapdoor? In a cemetery?'

'Yes, that's what I mean. What gave it away? The rings in the floor or the fact we're in a cemetery?'

Brian shone his torch down at the ring, put the bag on the floor and reached down, waited until Jackson had gripped his and they pulled together. It was a bit stiff, but they pulled harder and suddenly the trapdoor came free. Dust flew through the air and both men covered their mouths.

Jackson shone his torch down the concrete stairs.

'Where does it lead to?' Brian asked.

'To hell and back.' He shone the light in his

nephew's face. 'Or Shangri La, depending on whether your outlook on life is glass half empty or half full.'

'It looks dark down there.'

'It's in a cemetery, late at night in the middle of winter. Did you work that out all by yourself?'

'I'm just saying, I've had better Sunday nights.'

'And there will be more. Now get down those stairs.'

'You want me to go first?'

'Yes. If I trip and fall coming down behind you, I want a soft landing.'

'Oh, for fuck's sake.' Brian picked up the bag and started going down the concrete stairs. There was a wall on either side and the light disappeared into the gloom below. Then it showed a concrete landing. He stepped onto it and realised he was in an underground room. It opened up into a large space. Grave markers lined the walls on three sides. Most of them were old.

'See? It's not that scary,' Jackson said, joining him.

'What *is* this place?'

'This is the crypt itself. Upstairs is just for show. Down here is the business end.'

'It's freezing in here. Even colder than upstairs.'

'It's because it never gets any heat in here.' *Fucking halfwit.* Jackson kept the insult to himself. Now was a pivotal moment and he didn't want young Brian to go away in a huff, although he thought he would probably shoot the young man at this moment if he decided to jump ship.

'Uncle Adrian, I have to tell you, I'm shit scared. I don't know why we're down here, but I don't like it one bit.'

'You *will* like it, son. But I need you to promise me that what you see here will only be between you and me. Not even Rita can know. Yes, she'll get her cut, but what you see here is just for your eyes. Flesh and blood, remember. What do you say?'

'Sure. I promise. Just between you and me. But what about Fiona?'

'I'll tell Fiona when I'm ready. She doesn't know about this. I'll tell her in good time.'

Brian waved the light about the damp, cold room, his breath coming out like smoke. 'What's that doorway over there?'

'It leads out into the main crypt area. It's how they bring the coffins in. Why, did you think they slide them down the fucking steps?'

'I never thought.'

'Right, give me a hand.'

'What are we doing?'

'Just get that bag open.' Brian did as he was asked and Jackson took out a hammer and chisel. There was an array of tools, including screwdrivers and pliers. More chisels and hammers. Jackson pulled out two battery-operated LED lanterns. Small, but with a big kick.

'Get another hammer and chisel and start banging the surround of poor Aunty Mary over there.'

Brian did as he was told, and soon the night was filled with the banging and clanging that only a hammer meeting metal could make.

Jackson was the first one to chip the mortar away from around a grave marker set halfway up the wall.

'Half of these don't have any names on them,' Brian said.

'We're just doing the ones I say.'

Brian finished his and they stood looking at their handiwork in the cold, dusty air.

'Only four more to go, but let's get this one open first.' Jackson grabbed one edge of the marker while Brian grabbed the other and they pulled the stone away. Jackson grabbed a torch and shone it inside.

'Perfect!' he said when his eyes locked onto the contents.

THIRTY-SEVEN

Miller's nose had a plaster over it and his eyes were starting to go black.

Jeni Bridge had told him to take the day off as he wouldn't be any good to them going about moaning about how his face hurt. The Edward Hopkins murder was keeping them all busy.

He had a splitting headache as he looked down at his sleeping daughter. He was mesmerised by her looks. A little pink bundle, wrapped in her blanket. He gently stood up straight and quietly walked out of the room.

He had a splitting headache, but it wasn't just from being head-butted by a dead man. There was something buzzing about in his head. Something he didn't want to think but was blowing into his mind anyway.

'Frank, can I take Charlie when I go to see my dad in London?' Charlie was Miller's cat, now Emma's too.

'Honey, Charlie doesn't like going on the train. But Grandma will be taking you down, so you'll be fine.'

'Charlie will have to stay here and keep warm then,' Emma said.

'He'll miss you, sweetheart. And so will I.'

His stepdaughter rushed over to him and threw her arms round him. 'I'll miss you too, Frank. And if you get lonely, we can Facetime.'

'I look forward to that. I want to see my little princess before she goes to bed. And remember to take your teddy with you.'

She let him go. 'I will.'

The little girl forgot that her mother and new baby sister would be here with him.

Kim was in the shower and he made her a cup of coffee when she got out.

'You won't have to see Venus, now that the murder has been solved. You won't have to set foot in that hotel again.'

'Don't sound so smug. You know Robert Molloy and his clan are never far away. In fact, it was only a couple of years ago that your father wanted him lifted and sent down. Employing an undercover agent to work for Molloy. And that didn't work out, did it?'

'Why are you defending her? Why can't you just say, *I won't go near her, Kim?*'

'You're being paranoid.'

'No, I'm not.'

'I have paperwork to deal with,' he said, grabbing his coat from the rack in the hall. 'Bye Emma!'

'Bye, Frank!'

He walked out of the apartment, not knowing what to do anymore. But one thing he did know, he was going for a drive. He couldn't believe Kim was winding him up and it was only Monday morning.

He went downstairs and got into the Audi. Drove down to Queensferry Road and headed out of town. He marvelled at the new bridge, the Queensferry Crossing. He had applied to be one of the first people to walk over the bridge before it opened, but he and Kim hadn't been picked.

He took the exit for North Queensferry and drove along to Hillend. The little hamlet had been bypassed years ago, leaving the little street where the pub was located, quiet.

The Hillend Arms was like a little white, two-storey house. It looked very pleasant from the outside, with the snow on the roof. The wind was biting and the clouds were full of snow.

The opening hours were four pm until midnight. Miller looked at his watch; 9.57 am. He knocked on the door and a few minutes later, a burly man answered it.

'Can ye no' read?'

'I can read perfectly well, thanks,' Miller said, holding up his warrant card.

'Oh, right. I thought it was a friend o' Jock MacLean's, drunken old sod. Come away in. Ye want a coffee?'

'Thanks, that would be great.'

'Lorna! Two coffees!' he shouted through to the back and after a few minutes of comparing how cold it was in Edinburgh and Fife, a young woman brought two mugs through. The coffee had milk in it, which was fine.

'Now who's been making an arse of themselves? Pat Lynch?'

'No, nothing like that. I'm just looking for some information on a woman who used to live around here; Venus Molloy.'

'Venus, eh? That's a bit o' a fancy name for a young wench round here.'

'She said she drank in here often. She was dating somebody from here as well.' Miller took his phone out and showed the man the photo of Venus he'd taken of her covertly the other day when he had been in the hotel.

'Bonnie lass, but I've never seen her in here before.

You sure you got the right place? Not getting mixed up with Inverkeithing? They're all daft along there so it wouldn't surprise me.'

'No, she said she came from Fordell Gardens in Hillend.'

'Fordell? Most of the drinkers from up there come down here. Right bunch they are. Good laugh. Never have any problems with them, which is just as well, as they know what they would get if they started any o' their pish down here.'

'Where is Fordell from here?'

'Turn left at the end of the road here, drive straight up, and before you get to the bend in the road, there's a road on your right. The scouts have a place in there, but the rest is little roads with the mobiles on them.'

'Mobiles?'

'Mobile homes. Fordell Nurseries and Caravan Park it's called.'

'Thanks. And thanks for the coffee. You've been a great help.'

'Can I just ask you; what are the Edinburgh police doing over here? Why aren't the Fife polis not dealing with it?'

'I'm just looking for some information. I'm not here on official business.'

'Good luck, son. And if you're ever over here

looking for a hooly, we have a full house on a Saturday night.'

Miller got back in his car and followed the directions the bar owner had given him. At the top of the hill, he saw the bus stop and turned right into Fordell Gardens. There was a post with house numbers on it. He turned right into a narrow little road and followed it down.

The mobile homes were well kept, and Miller was pleasantly surprised. The one he was looking for was on the right-hand side, halfway down. There was a little parking area in front of the house and a car was in the driveway.

He got out and walked up to the front door and knocked. A young woman answered and looked at his warrant card as he introduced himself.

'Come in. It's freezing out there.'

The living room was warm and the place was immaculate.

'Nice house you have here,' he said, refusing her offer of a coffee.

'Technically, it's a double-wide but it has three bedrooms.'

There was a dining area to one side of the living room and a door leading off to another room. There was another area through the back that was being used as a TV area.

'I was just looking for information about a previous owner. Venus Molloy.'

'Previous owner? How long ago did she own this place?'

'Six months ago. Give or take. She and her mother had lived here for many years before that.'

'Have you got the right address?'

'Yes, why?'

'My husband's mother owned this place. She was here since 1985. She passed away and left it to us, so we done it up and moved out of our council house into here. It's great for the boys. They get their own room now.'

Miller looked puzzled. 'And you never rented to Venus or anything?'

'It's not a name you could forget. I've never heard of anybody by that name.'

'Maybe I did get the wrong number.'

'Even if you did, we've lived here for years and nobody by that name has ever lived here. It's a small community. Everybody knows everybody.'

Miller thanked her and left the house. Got back in his car and headed back to Edinburgh.

He knew where he had to go now.

THIRTY-EIGHT

Rita Mellon pulled the Jaguar in to the side of the road on the North Bridge and the van pulled in behind her.

'Keep the engine running, Rita. I want my bum warmer on for when I come back. Cold leather seats cause piles.'

Brian looked around the back where he was sitting. 'Fuck. I should have had mine on.'

'Let's go, son, and I'll show you the ropes.'

They got out of the car and four men got out of the van behind, big men wearing suits and leather gloves. They fell in line behind Jackson and Brian. The doors slid open and the entourage entered Molloy's hotel.

Jackson had his bowler hat back on and tapped his walking stick impatiently on the floor as he approached the desk and it took more than two seconds for the young woman to acknowledge him.

'I want to speak to Robert Molloy. If he's not out of his pit yet, wake him up.'

'Do you have an appointment?'

'Oh dear.' He looked round at Brian. 'Pay attention and you'll see how this works,' he said in a low voice, then to the girl, 'I don't need an appointment. My name's Adrian Jackson, and he'll piss his pants if I get turned away, so do yourself a favour and get on the blower to him.'

The girl obviously wanted to pass the buck and lifted the phone. Spoke into it and a minute later, a suited man appeared. Greg Sampson, Molloy's head of security.

'Mr Molloy will see you now,' Sampson said. 'The rest of you can stay here.'

'They're with me, son. They come with me. Molloy will understand. You got a problem with that, these gentlemen can show you the door.'

'Is that right?'

'Gentlemen, we don't want to start a pissing contest,' Venus Molloy said, coming into reception. 'Greg, take them upstairs.'

Sampson wasn't happy but led the way. He knocked on Robert Molloy's office door and showed Jackson in when he heard the shout.

'Stay here and watch the door,' Jackson said to the men. 'Brian, you come with me.'

The two men entered and the door closed behind them.

'I wondered when you would show your face round here,' Molloy said.

'Good seeing you again too, Robert. Any coffee on the go? It's such a cold day.'

'Who's this?'

'This young man is my nephew, Brian. I wanted to introduce him to you, so you recognise his face. He'll be working up through the ranks with me.'

Molloy laughed. 'You think you can just waltz back into Edinburgh and take back what was yours?'

'Yes.' Jackson walked across to the coffee maker and popped in a K cup. 'But don't you worry, Robert, I'm not after the club in George Street. You see, by the end of today, I will have all the properties back that were stolen from me by Peter Stanton.'

'And how do you intend to do that?' Molloy swivelled the office chair to look at him.

'Simple; he's going to sign them back over to me. I'm going to buy them back, of course, for exactly the same amount of money he paid for them, which was very little.'

'And he's going to do that, is he?'

'If he knows what's good for him, yes.'

'I bought some of your properties, too.'

Jackson sat down on a chair while Brian fiddled

with the coffee maker. 'You know the expression, *Pick your battles?* I chose not to go to battle with you, Robert. Yes, we work in the same business, but it's a matter of respect. Peter Stanton is a young pissant. His father was a wanker, a little thug. Peter is something to be crushed under my shoe. He doesn't have the same mettle as his father, although I give him ten out of ten for trying.'

Molloy smiled. 'And that's it? You're taking your properties back and going into the hospitality business?'

'I won't step on your toes. If you don't step on mine. We can co-exist. You, I've never had a problem with. Stanton, however, is a wannabe.'

'He took your properties without any problem. The profitable ones, anyway. Left your wife with the shitty boozers and the rental properties.'

'He took advantage of my wife. If it wasn't for her resolve, I would have had nothing left to come home to, so kudos to her.'

'But she's not as ruthless as you are, is that what you're saying?'

'That's exactly what I'm saying. I don't want to start a war, though I'm quite prepared to. But the glove was thrown down by the scumbag who posted me a letter, threatening me. I suspect it was Stanton, but I do not scare easily, Robert.'

'I appreciate your honesty. I don't see you as a threat, just like I didn't see Stanton as a threat. However, burning my son's house down was a wee bit cheeky, just to get your point across. And I might be forgiving, but my son is certainly not.'

Jackson looked Molloy in the eyes. 'I give you my word, that was nothing to do with me. If I wanted to make a point, I would have burned down the club in George Street, not your son's house. What's the point in that?'

Molloy nodded. 'You're saying Stanton is responsible?'

'I'm saying, *I'm* not responsible. I'm not a stupid man, Robert. What would be the point of starting a war with you? Things would escalate out of control pretty quickly and it's not something we would come back from. After twenty-five years in prison, I want to have a good life. A *quiet* life.'

'I see I'll have to speak with Stanton. I can't let him make an arse of me. However, you could just be pitching me against him, to suit your own ends.'

'I could, but I'm not. I'm a man of my word. If that was my game, I wouldn't come here and talk to you about it. I'd light the blue touch paper and sit back. But if you're intending to talk to him, you should know I'm going to see him this morning. I want my properties back. If you do intend to have a chat with him, I'd like it if this was *after* I've had my chat.'

'Fair enough. But let me warn you, if I find out you're trying to fuck me over, you'll have a war whether you like it or not.'

Jackson stood up. 'I look forward to seeing you at the next Rotary Club meeting.' He walked out of the office before Brian had a chance to put milk in his coffee.

THIRTY-NINE

The black Range Rover was waiting on the North Bridge for Kim. One of the bodyguards got out and helped her load the car seat into the back and strap it in. Emma was already away to school.

The big car moved off and did a U-turn and turned left into the High Street before going down St Mary's Street.

Her father's office was only five minutes away. He had a basement section of the new Scottish Parliament building and the car went through the security barriers and into the underground car park.

She carried the baby in her seat to the lift and went up one level and along to her father's office.

'Well, this is a nice surprise on a Monday morning,' Neil McGovern said. 'How's my cheeky wee girl this morning?' He smiled at his new granddaughter.

'I'm fine, thanks, Dad.'

'I was talking to the little one.'

'I know you were. It was sarcasm.'

'Put her down next to the couch,' he said. 'I'll get us a coffee.'

He left the office and Kim put Annie down beside the leather couch and took her coat off and hung it on the coat rack. Sat down. And burst into tears.

McGovern came back with the two coffees and put them on his desk. 'Kim, whatever's the matter?' He sat down beside his daughter and put his arm around her shoulders.

'Life, Dad. Life's the matter.' She stopped sobbing. 'Sometimes I hate my life.'

'You know we have a father-daughter bond and you can tell me anything. If you don't want me to mention it to your mother, I won't.' Which wasn't quite true; if it was something that was detrimental to Kim's well-being, then he would run it past Norma.

She rubbed her eyes. 'I just feel hacked off all the time. I don't think Frank loves me anymore.'

'Listen, Kim, women's emotions are all over the place when they have a new baby. It's natural. Of course Frank loves you. I mean, I'm not dismissing your feelings, but if there's one man who loves you, it's Frank.'

'Look at Eric, though, Dad; he ended up having an affair after Emma was born.'

'He was under a lot of stress. He's with the SAS and if there's one job that carries a lot of stress, that's it.'

'Frank is too. And he's going to be under a lot more stress when I do what I want to do.'

'You're not going to do anything silly I hope.'

'No, nothing like that. But ever since Venus came into his life, he's been seeing her more and more.'

'Socially?'

'No, but through work.'

'It's understandable. And yes, I know she looks almost exactly like his wife, but it's not as though he was pursuing her.'

'He was chasing her last summer.'

'I'm just playing Devil's Advocate here, but look at it from his point of view; he thought he was seeing his dead wife. Turns out it was her twin sister that he didn't know about. And she is Robert Molloy's daughter. She's going to be around.'

'I know, I'm a jealous cow. But I did something stupid this morning.'

'I'm listening.'

'I tracked Frank's phone. He drove over to Fife. Where she comes from.'

'I thought she lived here now?'

'She does. But why would he go over there?'

'I don't know, Kim. How are you going to ask him?'

'I'm not.' She shook her head and took a deep breath. 'My gut instinct is telling me there's something wrong.'

'In what way?'

'I know she showed Molloy her birth certificate. Frank was there at the time. I mean, Molloy wasn't just going to take her word for it. But it was something Frank said, an off-the-cuff remark that I started thinking about recently. He said, and we were arguing at the time, *I saw it for myself! The crispy new birth certificate proving she is who she is.* I have my birth certificate in my fire safe. It isn't crispy and new. It's old and you can tell it's been handled.'

'I see what you're getting at; why would somebody have a brand new one?'

'I want to do some checking, Dad. I need your help.'

'I'll call Ian Powers. He's my best IT man.'

FORTY

Larry Cresswell was like a kid when it came to Christmas. He had to admit, because he was the only child, his parents had spoiled him. Birthdays, Christmas, Easter. He was showered with gifts. Scramble was different; his father was a drunk who beat him when he was a kid. That was why he had run away to join the army.

Larry didn't rub Scramble's nose in the fact that he had wanted for nothing at Christmas. It didn't stop him getting excited though. Constance had known this and had jumped right on board. They had showered each other with gifts and it had been a special day for them.

That was why he'd got excited when Scramble said they should splash out on each other this year since they were making a lot of money. They were the best of friends as well as colleagues, so it didn't hurt to buy stuff.

Larry's excitement got the better of him. Less than a week to go and he wanted to know what Scramble had bought for him. He wasn't going to look at them all. He would maybe just peek at one thing. Ease the paper back, peel the tape away, and look at it without opening the box. It had worked for him when he was a kid, and it worked now. Last year, Scramble had gotten him a radio-controlled pick-up truck and he had played with it in their back garden.

He trudged through the snow. There would be no radio-controlled cars playing in the garden this year. Snow had come early, buggering things up. He walked round the plumber's van and up to the garage door. He opened it. It was huge, big enough to put both their vehicles in, but their landlord kept all his shite in here. Old tools, lawnmowers, you name it, if it could go rusty, it came here to die.

A shaft of light hit some of the old machines. He made his way to the left where there was a rough path to walk through all the garbage. He was careful not to get caught on any of the sharp pieces and end up with tetanus. If that happened, he would be visiting the landlord in the middle of the night in his plumber's van. And Larry would insert a U-bend up his jacksy.

He managed to get to the back of the large garage

without killing himself on an errant hand-push lawn-mower and saw the old sheet covering his presents against the back wall in one corner.

The excitement was almost too much to bear.

By the size of it, it looked like Scramble had pulled out all the stops. Larry grabbed hold of the sheet and pulled it.

Being a contract killer, he had a tolerance for gore that the man in the street might not have, but the sight before him made him jump back a little.

His ex-wife, Constance Britain, sat in a heap in the corner. The axe had dried blood on it, but it no longer resembled blood. It almost looked like rust.

The tool had sliced into the front of her skull, severing her left eye and leaving her brain exposed.

Larry took a few deep breaths. He knew *who* had killed her but didn't know *why*. One thing was for sure, his partnership with Scramble had just ended.

'Thanks for meeting me, Bruce,' Lou Purcell said.

'No problem.' They were standing outside the Apple store on Princes Street. 'Are you ready to go up?'

Lou nodded. 'I'm feeling nervous, to be honest.'

'That's to be expected.'

They walked up the lane, past the General

Register House to New Register House at the back. Inside, they welcomed the heat. They approached a counter and told the man what they wanted. They had booked a session, so they were shown through to the reading room and sat down at one of the desks that ran round the perimeter of the large room.

Hagan showed Lou how to navigate through the computer and they eventually found the death certificate for Thomas Young. It was registered by a woman.

'Wait a sec and I'll find the obituary online,' Hagan said, taking his phone out. Technically Amanda's phone since she was paying for it.

'Here it is. Since he was a judge, they ran a fancy obit in *The Caledonian*. It says here he had two daughters. No mention of any sons.'

'My mother distinctly told me I had two brothers. Why would she say that?'

'I have no idea, Lou. It does say here that he had two nephews. Thomas had a younger brother called George. Now we've got their names, we can look them up at the National Library of Scotland where they keep the names of registered voters.'

'Can we go there now?'

'Of course we can, Lou. But let's not be hasty. We can see what family members are still alive.'

They searched some more until they got the answers.

As they were leaving and walking down the steps into the staff car park, they bumped into Frank Miller.

'Frank! What are you doing here?' Lou said.

'Just doing some family research.' Miller looked at Hagan. 'Hi, Bruce.'

'Now you really are making me feel paranoid,' Hagan said, smiling.

'Don't be, my friend. I'm here on private business.' Frank walked past the two men and on into the building.

FORTY-ONE

'He's going to ruin me, Chrissie! I thought you were going to get rid of him? A couple of days, you said! A couple of fucking days! You hired somebody to burn down Molloy's house. They should have been at each other's throats. And nothing. What the hell is going on?'

'I have to go to work. Don't do anything stupid.'

'That's your answer? I'm going to be royally fucked, you know that?'

'As I said, don't do anything stupid.'

'Christ, my dad screwed Jackson out of some of his boozers. What the hell are we going to do now?'

'A few crappy little holes. One in Niddrie, one in Longstone and one in the south side. If he wants them back, give them to him. Make sure you make a profit.'

'Okay.' Peter Stanton didn't have what his father had when it came to dealing with people. Yes, he'd intimidated Fiona Jackson, but when it came to the likes of dealing with Adrian Jackson, he knew he didn't have it. The peace they'd had for the last twenty-five years was gone. His father had been around for the first seven years of Jackson being in prison, but then his heart had given out and the reins had been handed to Peter. And Peter didn't like it one bit. His ex-wife had been far stronger, and he sometimes yearned for the old days. Meeting Chrissie had been wonderful; she had been as tough as Peter's father.

He had missed her when she had been gone for those few months, and he had been excited when she came back, but now she had changed mentally. Like something had switched in her head as well. He wanted the old Chrissie back, but he knew she wasn't coming back.

She came back out of their bedroom with a light jacket on. 'And when we're done with this, we can see about moving to Trinity.'

'My ex will never move out of there.'

'Maybe she won't have to.' She kissed him on the cheek.

'What are you talking about?'

'See you later.' She left the apartment.

Adrian Jackson was playing with the radio in his Jag. Stopped tuning when he got to a classical station.

'What's this pish?' Brian asked.

Rita laughed. 'Brian prefers some house music or something.'

Jackson looked round at his nephew. 'Is that right? Whatever the fuck *house* music is.'

'It's where some DJ makes a lot of noise,' Brian said. 'It's not for old farts.'

'I had plenty of noise where I was, son. You learn to appreciate the peace and quiet.' He fiddled with the radio again until he got to the local radio station.

'*...Police are not revealing the name of the murder victim until the next of kin can be reached. They have no suspects at this time, but if you were in the vicinity of Russell Place last night, in the area of Trinity, and saw something suspicious, police would like to speak to you...*'

'That's a coincidence. Peter Stanton's ex lives in Russell Place,' Jackson said, turning the volume down.

'Do you think it's her?'

'It wouldn't surprise me. There's been some shady things going on since I got back and no mistake.'

He looked over to one of the front doors for the

apartments when a taxi pulled up. He watched the woman come out and get into the taxi.

'That's very interesting.'

Rita and Brian looked over like a couple of kids being driven through a safari park.

'That is indeed,' Rita said. 'I saw her earlier this morning.'

'Right, time to go. Rita, keep the old girl running.'

'I know; bum warmers.'

'Correct.' He turned to Brian. 'It's payday for you both. Don't fuck up.'

He got out of the car and put his bowler hat on. Brian followed. Jackson waved his walking stick to the driver of the van behind.

The driver turned around and spoke to somebody and then the side door was opening and four men stepped out, each carrying a holdall.

'This way, boys,' he said, leading them into the stairway.

They rode the lift up to the level they wanted. Peter Stanton was waiting for Jackson.

'I hope you've got the kettle on, old son. I'm parched.'

Stanton made a face and walked into the living room.

'No? Never mind. I just had a coffee from the

coffee shop downstairs.' Jackson sat down on one of the leather chairs. *His* chair now.

'We're just waiting for my friend,' he said. 'Brian, how do you like this place?'

'It's nice.'

'What a difference twenty-five years makes. The old hospital turned into flats and more built on the land. I was born in Simpson's maternity, but that's gone now too. Progress, I suppose.'

The door buzzer rang. 'Go and answer that,' Jackson said to one of the men. The suit did as he was told and a moment later, Richard Sullivan, Jackson's lawyer, appeared.

'And now we're all here. Oh, and I saw your companion leave. Does she know what's going on?'

'No. Not all of it. She thinks I'm just selling you a few scabby old pubs.'

'She'll be pissed off when she finds out that you have nothing left.'

'Look, can we just be civil about this?' Stanton looked like a schoolboy who's just had his ball stolen by the bully.

'I thought I was being civil. You see, you forced my Fiona to sell our properties for a song. Then you ripped off the ones you left her with. You took my properties for pennies on the pound, Peter. Ripped me right off. So now you're going to sell them back to me.'

'Should I have my lawyer here?'

'You can if you want. But that would mean you'll both be leaving here in bin liners.'

'Christ, you're saying that in front of your own lawyer.'

Jackson turned to Sullivan. 'Did you hear that?'

'Hear what?'

Jackson smiled as he turned back to Stanton. 'He has selective hearing. It goes with the bank balance I'm about to swell. Now, you see those bags? They have cash in them. Enough to cover our transaction. You will sign the paperwork, I will give you the cash and you will leave Edinburgh. Whether you tell your woman, that's up to you.'

'Let's get on with it.'

'Was it you who sent that note to me? The threatening letter?'

'No, it was her.'

Jackson nodded to the first man who walked forward with the bag of money and tipped it out on the dining table. The other three bags were emptied onto the leather couch.

'The pubs, the clubs, the hotel in George Street, and this place. This is all mine now.'

'Not this place, surely?'

'I know it wasn't mine, but let's call it interest. And

think yourself lucky I don't have you thrown off the balcony afterwards.'

'Christ, you're bleeding me dry.'

'Now you know how it feels.' Jackson watched Sullivan go through the paperwork.

'Does your girlfriend own half of this place?'

'She doesn't even own the little sports car in the car park downstairs.'

'Sports car?'

'Well, it's a Porsche Boxster.'

'Right, I'll have that too. I know somebody who could use a new car.'

'For fuck's sake.'

After half an hour, Peter Stanton was without properties. And a car.

'I have nothing now.'

'You have four bags of money. Greedy bastard. However, I suggest you get the fuck out of here before your fancy piece gets back. She's bad news.'

'She's not that bad.'

'I heard on the radio that a woman was found dead in Russell Place this morning. Murdered. Didn't your ex live there?'

Stanton looked at him. 'Yes.'

'Ask your girlfriend where she was last night. Or if she didn't leave the apartment, look at whatever secret bank accounts you have and see if there's been any big withdrawals recently. Hitmen don't come cheap.'

'She wouldn't.'

'Don't turn your back on her, Stanton.'

'She'll come after you.'

'Listen, son, cut your losses now and put some distance between yourself and this mess. It ends now. If you stay, you'll get caught in the crossfire. I'm here to stay and anybody who gets in my way will not survive. Got that? Do yourself a favour and leave. If somebody took out a hit on your ex-wife, what's to say they're not coming for you next?'

Five minutes later, Peter Stanton had packed a suitcase and called for a taxi. He put the money in another large suitcase and left without saying goodbye.

Jackson laughed. 'Big bonuses all round. I'll have to call my cousin and thank him. He's sending some guys up from London to be my permanent staff. Heavily vetted, all ex special forces. Life is going to be good, Brian. And now you can live here, with or without Rita, but she's staying on my staff. How about you?'

'I think I could manage that.'

Jackson turned to the four bodyguards. 'See that Brian gets safely down to the car and wait for me there.'

The men trooped out. Jackson turned to Sullivan. 'There must be some of the good stuff here.'

Sullivan found a good bottle of whisky. 'I don't know how you did it, but you did it. Bought back your places.'

'They were mine to begin with.'

'I know, but it still cost you a pretty penny.'

'It cost me nothing, Richard. Stanton's old man stashed a load of money, gold coins, and jewellery in the family crypts. Young Peter there followed suit. My Fiona followed them one night. And God bless her, she went in there, by herself no less, and saw they had opened up another crypt. The mortar was wet. When she told me this, I knew he was doing the same thing as his old man. So last night, me and my boy there, we emptied it.'

'You took his money?'

'Every last penny. And everything else. What Peter Stanton has there is his own cash.'

Sullivan laughed. 'He'll find out soon enough if he goes to make a deposit. Or a withdrawal.'

'I had a team go in there and vandalise the place. Graffiti, smash the place up. They opened up the crypts and took one of the coffins out. It looks like some hooligans found the hiding place and stole everything.'

'He'll never believe the coincidence.'

'Why not? It's not as if I know he has a hiding place down there, is it?'

Sullivan smiled again and they clinked glasses. 'How did you get him to sign the papers?'

'I told him that Robert Molloy would wipe him off the face of the earth. Especially when he finds out who Stanton's girlfriend is.'

'Her name's Chrissie Green, isn't it?'

'Yes, it is. But that's not how Robert Molloy knows her.'

FORTY-TWO

Larry watched as the Land Rover Discovery came into the snow-covered driveway with confidence. The small man got out and came in through the kitchen door. Larry stood waiting.

'I picked up something nice for lunch. A nice, steak and kid—'

He stopped when he saw Larry sitting in the chair with a shotgun pointed at him.

'Jesus, what are you doing? That fucking thing might go off. That's what my last girlfriend said as well, mind.'

'Why did you do it, Scramble?'

The smaller man's smiling face faltered for a second. 'Do what?'

'Please. We've known each other too long for this bullshit.'

'I had to! She was going to come here! Some twat had been murdered at the hotel, and I thought the police would come crawling round here.'

'They came because she was missing! You took Constance, killed her and because she was missing, they came here looking for information! Can you see the irony?'

'Admittedly, I didn't plan it through properly.'

'You killed her.' There were tears running down Larry's face now. 'Everything's up in the air now. We're on the police radar and I lost the love of my life.'

'Larry, listen to yourself! Constance was married to somebody else. She wasn't interested in you.'

'That's not true! That letter I got the other day? She said she wanted to reconnect with me. I would have loved that. She's the only woman I ever loved.'

'I know. I read it! How do you think I knew she was going to come here? You said you hated her.'

'My *first* wife! Not Constance! Don't you ever fucking listen?'

'Oh, I thought you meant the second one.'

'No, not the second one. The second one was the good one.'

'I'll make it up to you, Larry. I'll buy you a Land Rover.'

'What's the point of all this now? I thought the

extra money would be good for me and Constance to start again.'

'I'm sorry, pal. I messed up.'

'Sit down.'

Scramble sat down in the comfy armchair. 'So what do we do now?'

Frank Miller walked up the North Bridge from Register House. He felt empty inside, like somebody had hollowed him out and thrown away the contents.

He held onto his phone, not quite being able to let it go after the call he'd received. It was as if the news just cemented what he'd been sure of but didn't know for a fact.

The caller had just filled in the gaps.

The wind was wicked as it shot over from the east side, hitting him in the face as it brought snow with it. His thoughts were predominantly of Carol. He would often wonder what they would have been doing together and now he thought about their first Christmas together, how happy they were in their flat down in Comely Bank.

Now he was married to Kim and he wished that she trusted him more. Maybe she would trust him more from now on. After today.

He reached Molloy's hotel and went into the lobby. Venus was there.

'Hi, Frank! How are you?'

'Cold.'

'You want a coffee?'

'That would be great. But I need to see Robert and Michael.'

'Oh? I hope nothing's wrong?'

'Just wrapping up the case.'

'Your face looks sore.'

'It'll ease up.'

'You go on up and I'll get somebody to call ahead. Then I'll bring you a coffee.'

'You know what? Just come up with me. I think you'll want to hear this.'

'This has been a hell of a weekend.'

'Tell me about it.'

They got in the lift and got out on the office level. Venus walked along in front of Miller and knocked on Robert Molloy's door.

'Come!'

They stepped inside. 'Dad, Frank Miller is here to speak—'

She stopped when she saw Adrian Jackson sitting there. Michael Molloy was sitting on a chair, his father behind the desk.

'Oh, I'm sorry. I didn't realise you had a guest.'

'It's fine. Show Frank in.'

Miller and Venus stepped into the office.

'Could you make us some coffee from my machine, please?' Robert said, smiling. 'Frank! Good job on catching that nutter. People will be concentrating on Christmas the next few days, and not thinking about that arsehole.'

Miller closed the door behind him as Venus walked over to the Keurig machine. He noticed that Greg Sampson was over to one side and the big bouncer stepped over to the door.

Miller stood at the end of the couch. 'You know what, Venus, maybe you could just join us,' Miller said.

She turned round. 'Is everything okay?' She eyed Sampson but stayed where she was.

Miller looked at Molloy and Jackson and they both nodded. 'You know, things happen in life. Somebody says something, does something, that sparks a question. I was talking to somebody who told me he was going to look into his ancestors because he just found out he was adopted when he was a child. It got me thinking.'

'Thinking about what, Frank?' She had a worried look on her face now.

'You.'

'Me?' Now a puzzled look but it seemed fake.

'You'd shown Robert your birth certificate, hadn't you?' He looked at Molloy, who nodded again.

'I wanted to make sure he believed I was who I said I was.'

'Even though you look exactly like Carol.'

'What are you getting at?'

'You came into my life, deliberately making sure I saw you and like a fool, I chased after you. Then you wheedled your way into Robert Molloy's life and after losing Carol he is so elated at having a daughter that he didn't know he had, become part of his life, that he offers you a job. You accept and get an apartment. And you live happily ever after.'

'You're not making sense.'

'Venus Molloy doesn't exist.'

'I fucking knew it!' Michael Molloy said, barely able to contain himself.

'What are you talking about?' said Venus.

'I drove over to Fife and spoke to the person who lives in the mobile home you said your mother owned. It's a small enough community that they would have known you well. Nobody knows who you are. I checked your mother's birth certificate and every other certificate I could think of, and nothing. Then I got a call from Mr Jackson there.'

'I saw you coming out of the apartment building before I went up to speak to Peter Stanton,' Jackson said to her.

'I have to admit; the plastic surgery gives you a

remarkable likeness to Carol. It must have cost a pretty penny,' Miller said. 'The surgeon must have been very skilled to change you into Venus from being Chrissie Green.'

'You should have just let me deal with her, Dad,' Michael said.

'Give it a rest. I feel foolish enough as it is.'

'It did cost a lot. Even though the guy had been struck off, he still does pretty good work in Spain, with an excellent team. If you have the money, of course,' said Venus.

'Why would you be so desperate to get in with the Molloys?' Miller said, 'and who killed your accountant?'

'You lot haven't got a clue, have you?'

'Cheeky cow,' Michael said, getting up out of the chair.

That's when Venus brought the gun out from behind her back. 'Sit down, arsehole. I knew as soon as that prick came in here that something was up.' She indicated Jackson. 'This whole thing started when we read about him getting released. We knew we had a few months, so I made a plan with Peter. All we had to do was get me in here to gain their confidence and then pitch Jackson against Molloy so they would destroy each other.'

'It didn't quite go to plan, did it?' Jackson said, smiling. He stood up.

'Sit down!'

'Sorry, love, no can do. I have a torn disk in my lower back and it gives me sciatica. Shoot if you must, but I have to stretch my back. And since I have this injury, I am no threat to you. But please, do carry on.'

'I wanted Michael's house burnt down and Peter's ex-wife killed. I had to get rid of the accountant to divert suspicion away from us, and I never trusted him anyway, but I didn't tell Peter. It was better if he thought that you were coming after us at well, so that he would stick with the plan. I wanted you going after each other, so Peter and I would rule Edinburgh. The Jacksons and the Molloys, all gone. And now you had to meddle in it before the hitmen took you out,' she said to Miller.

'This is all very well, but I really could do with a spot of tea. Do you have a kettle around somewhere, Robert?' Jackson said.

'Are you for real?' Venus said.

'I am, Chrissie, yes. Very real.' He leant heavily on his walking stick. 'Tell me though; what do you plan to do now that Peter sold all of his businesses to me? The ones his father practically stole from me?'

'You mean the little shitty boozers in Niddrie? You can keep them. That doesn't bother us.'

'Oh dear. Obviously, Peter wasn't quite truthful; he sold me everything. Including the hotel in George Street. And the apartment in Quartermile. He has nothing. That's why he's left the city. There's nothing here for him now. And that's why Robert and I will be working side by side, with an understanding. And you, my dear, are fucked.'

'I'll kill you all. If what you say is true, I've nothing to lose.'

'Who are the hitmen?' Miller said.

'Oh, you would love to know that, wouldn't you? Because they're after you now. But that's not how it works. That's the beauty of the internet. The dark web. You can hire killers and as long as you pay the money, you don't even have to know who they are. The two of them have your name, Miller, and I can't call them off.'

'It is what it is,' Miller said with a confidence he didn't feel.

'I'll be going now. But you know I can't let you all live. It's just a case of who's going to die first. I think it should be you, Robert.'

As she turned towards Molloy, Jackson pulled the sword out of his walking stick in one fluid movement and put the point of it at her throat before she could fire.

'Drop it on the floor,' he said.

She did and held up her hands.

'Okay, you win, Jackson,' Venus said.

Miller got up and picked up the gun. 'Chrissie Green, I'm arresting you-'

Like a lot of incidents, this one happened so suddenly, it took a few seconds to react.

Venus Molloy, AKA Chrissie Green, reached round to her back and brought out a second, smaller pistol. Miller saw it in her hand and it was almost as if the action was in slow motion. He saw her spinning towards him as he was the one with the gun and she wanted it back.

Miller brought the first gun up and hesitated for a split second. It was like taking aim on his wife Carol, but he knew this wasn't Carol, nor her twin as she didn't have one. This woman was an imposter, who'd made herself look like Carol for the sole purpose of deceiving Malloy, and she was about to kill them all.

He fired the gun and the bullet caught Venus in the side of the head and she jerked and fell down.

The men stood around looking at each other, the gunshot deafening in the room.

'Pretty nice shot, actually,' Adrian Jackson said, and they all breathed a collective sigh of relief.

Robert Molloy looked down at the dead woman. 'It was nice having a daughter again, even if it was only for a few months.'

'How in God's name am I going to write this in a report?' Miller said.

'Oh, I think you've got more things to worry about,' Jackson said. 'Like a pair of hitmen.'

FORTY-THREE

Reports of a shot fired brought out the Armed Response Vehicle. The two armed officers gained entry to the house just outside Ratho without incident.

They cleared the house and found two dead males, one with what looked like a self-inflicted shotgun blast. The back of his head was splattered across one of the living room walls, and no doubt there was other blood spatter, but that was for the techs to find. The shotgun was being cradled in his arm, where it had fallen after he had put it under his chin and pulled the trigger.

The other dead man was lying on the kitchen floor.

'What a fucking smell,' the lead officer said. 'Christ, it's like a farm in here.'

'He must have gone off his nut or something,' the second one said. 'Killed his pal and then couldn't face the music. Something like that?'

'You don't know what goes through their minds when they're about to off themselves. Maybe he found out that Tesco's been selling their turkey's cheap after he already bought his.'

'It's the worst time of year for suicides. Christmas. Some people can't handle the pressure. Me? I buy the wife some sexy new lingerie out of Markies and Bob's your aunt fanny.'

'What? Away with yourself. Your Linda wants you to buy her undies at the Gyle?'

'A man can dream.' He stepped away from the cooling corpse of Scramble and got on the radio. Called it in. Area secure. Two. Life extinct.

It didn't need a doctor to tell them they were both dead, but the duty doc would be called out anyway, just to make it official.

The first officer went to the front door and gave the all clear. Then the uniforms who had been out of sight came in. And then the circus started.

They knew not to touch anything as the forensics team would be on their way, but the first armed officer stood looking down at a piece of paper on the kitchen table.

Written at the top were two words: HIT LIST. Names had been scored out. Except for two.

'I think these two names were lucky,' he said to his friend. 'Looks like those guys were hitmen.'

'Jesus. Maybe they got into a fight. One killed his pal, then decided to take his own life.'

The first one shrugged. 'Shit happens.'

'Christ, this is a bit of a comedown from a house in the New Town,' Lou Purcell said from the passenger seat.

They had stopped outside a block of flats in Niddrie. 'It's different, I'll give you that,' Hagan said.

'I'm sure there are some nice people living here, but they don't have graffiti on their front doors in Moray Place.'

They got out of the car and walked up to the stair entryway and went inside. The ground floor flat they were looking for was on the left. Lou looked at Hagan before knocking. Hagan nodded and Lou rapped his knuckles on the wood.

A haggard-looking woman who could be anywhere from in her forties to in her sixties answered the door.

'What the fuck do you want?'

'My name's Lou Purcell. I've been doing family research and I got a name; Barry McGuire. Does he still live here?'

'Barry! Get your arse out here. Some old ponce looking for you.'

'Fuck me,' Hagan said, under his breath.

'Fuckin polis again. What do you lot want now?' The man they assumed was Barry said as he appeared at the door.

'We're not police. I'm trying to trace some ancestors.'

'Ancestors? I didn't know I had any.'

Hagan looked at the scruffy man, could see the wheels turning in his head; maybe there was money to be had from this old geezer.

'I think I might be related to Thomas Young, the judge who used to live in Moray Place.'

'None of my family used to live there.'

'Are you sure?'

'Of course I'm sure. Hey, Betty, do you remember my maw saying anything about Moray Place?'

'Aye. Your grandfather used to deliver coal there. Back in the fifties. Dirty old bastard, your mother said. Her father would ride anything he could get his hands on. He even got a scullery maid up the stick and the judge went off his nut. The young lassie had to leave because of your grandfather.'

'Oh aye, I remember that now!' Barry chuckled and lit another cigarette. 'And you're my ancestor?'

'Not sure if you're the ancestor or not,' Lou said, feeling his stomach drop.

'Well, if he left me millions in his will, be sure to

come back!' Barry and Betty were both chuckling as they shut the door.

Back in the car, Lou brought the letter out again, read it through and passed it over to Bruce. 'How could I have got it so wrong?'

Hagan scanned the letter again. 'Lou, it just says here that she worked for the judge. Your father had two boys. It doesn't actually say the judge was your father.'

'Christ, in my excitement, I got carried away.' He shook his head and looked out at the snow that had started falling again. 'You should think about becoming a private investigator, son. I think you would be good at it.'

Hagan handed the letter back. 'You think so?'

'You were a good cop. Your skills are going to waste.'

'I'll give it some thought. You could come and work with me. I don't trust many people nowadays, but I trust you, Lou.'

'The boys are back in town, eh? But wait; Percy's going to laugh his head off when he finds out my mother was shagging a coalman who used to deliver the coal to the big house.'

Hagan shrugged. 'Don't tell him, then. Say you couldn't find anybody still alive. Case closed.'

'You might be on to something there.'

Hagan started the car up and they drove away.

FORTY-FOUR

'It's a murder-suicide,' Purcell said as he and Miller pulled up to the loading bay entrance of the mortuary.

'Christ, what a week,' Miller said, leaving the warmth of the car, like a baby leaves the womb, into the cold, harsh reality of winter.

'It's certainly been all go, that's for sure.'

Gus Weaver let them in to the mortuary. 'I hope you didn't go to too much expense for my Christmas gift,' Miller said to him.

'You already told me you weren't expecting anything, and now you hope I didn't spend a lot. Boy, as friends go, you take the ticket.'

'What you're saying is, you got me nowt.'

'Exactly.'

'If you were any more tight, your arse would squeak when you walk,' Purcell said.

'Charming. I'm going to take yours back, just for that.'

'You got me something? Really?'

'Yes, and it's not too late to take it back to Pound Savers.'

'Don't be calling me the next time you get a speeding ticket, Weaver.'

'As if. This way, gents.'

They went upstairs to the post-mortem suite where the two bodies were laid out on the steel tables.

Professor Leo Chester was there, with Kate Murphy and Jake Dagger. 'And now we complete the picture of the motley crew,' Purcell said.

'Ah, Percy! Just the man I wanted to see. Are you up for coming along to the Christmas hooly on Thursday?'

'Count me in, doc. I know you need faces to make up the numbers. Young Frank here likes to give it a good belting. What say you, Frank?'

Miller was staring at the two bodies. 'These two are from the house in Ratho, yes?'

'Yes, this is the pair who we think was doing the jobs for Venus Molloy, even though she said she wasn't directly involved,' Purcell said. 'There was a list of names in the kitchen. It had *Hit list* written on top. Your name was there, apparently.'

'I know that. Venus said my name was on their list.'

He looked at Purcell. 'What other names were on the list?'

'Wait, I'll get Maggie Parks to send me through a photo of it.' He walked to the side and sent a text message.

'This isn't them,' Miller said.

'What do you mean?' Purcell said.

'Sir, this isn't them.'

'Yes, it is. The one with his face blown off had a driving license in his wallet. The other we assumed was Larry Cresswell. He had a letter addressed to him on the kitchen table, along with a bunch of letters.'

'He's badly decomposed.'

'We think the short one offed him earlier in the week, then decided to kill himself. We're having their prints run right now, but there's no reason to believe that it's not them. Is there?'

Miller looked at Dagger. 'What are their heights?'

'Decompose is five foot eight. Face blown off is five foot five.'

'Christ, maybe one of them is there, but the other guy isn't. Constance Britain's ex-husband is around, six-four, six-five and built like a brick shithouse. He's not one of those guys.'

'Christ,' Purcell said, 'that means he's still out there.'

His phone dinged and he looked at the list of names. 'God almighty, Frank, we have to go!'

FORTY-FIVE

Make it look like an accident. That was the instruction. Larry Cresswell had called their handler again and told him that Scramble was no longer with us, that he had moved on to a better place.

The handler had told him to call back and ten minutes later, he had new instructions; death by any means. As long as they were dead, that's all that mattered, and he could have Scramble's share.

With Scramble's share, he would ditch this van and get a Land Rover. He had to admit, the Discovery's heated seats were far better than his Transit's.

He was sitting on Cockburn Street, the engine running, waiting. The black Audi was sitting opposite, down the hill a bit. He had it fixed in his sights. The radio was playing some classical stuff, which helped soothe him. His feelings were all over the place, what with the death of Constance and having to kill Scramble. But business was business. Two more people, then he was off.

Then the lights flashed on the Audi. He looked at the arcade, which ran through from the North Bridge to Cockburn Street, a shortcut for Kim Smith if she was going to the car. And there she was. Blondie, walking to the car holding the baby in the car seat.

He wouldn't touch the kid. If they were somewhere quiet when he killed its mother, he would drop it off somewhere safe. Play it by ear.

Blondie put the car seat in the back, climbed in the front and pulled away. Larry followed a few cars behind.

The car turned right at the bottom of the road. When it was his turn, he followed and saw her driving along Market Street, past the back entrance to Waverley Station. The lights changed and the cars moved forward. She was only two cars in front, but he slowed down. Not that the van would draw attention, but the roads were still wet with the snow lying in the gutters.

The Audi got to the end of the road, past the new hotel on the right and the council buildings on the left and she turned left to go down New Street.

The cars behind turned left and then a bin truck reversed down New Street, blocking his path. The men got out and went to the back and pushed a black communal bin to the back.

'Come on, for fuck's sake.' Larry almost leant on the horn but didn't want to draw attention to himself.

Then the men were back in the truck and it moved out of the way.

Larry turned left and headed down the hill the same way the Audi had gone. He didn't see it.

He drove as fast as he could to the bottom of the hill. This part of the road went under a railway bridge, carrying train tracks into Waverley Station. He looked left and saw it. The car had been stopped at a temporary red traffic light, the exhaust fumes swirling in the cold air.

Luckily for Larry, there were always road works somewhere in Edinburgh. He pulled the van round and drove up to the car and he jumped out. He didn't take his gun out just yet in case he spooked her.

The car had tinted windows in the back so maybe she wouldn't be able to see him well either. He walked up to the car. This would be like a carjacking gone wrong. He would take her purse, just to make it look good.

No cars were coming through the road works from the opposite direction. Nothing coming up Calton Road from the Holyrood end. Nothing else coming down New Street. Vans were parked on the other side of the street but no workmen were near them.

He looked around, grabbed the door handle, not expecting it to be open but prepared to shoot through the glass, but the door did open.

There was nobody in the driver's seat. The car seat was empty. He ducked in, looking around. What the hell was going on?

'It's over, Larry!' he heard a voice shout. He stood up straight. A man was in the middle of the road, walking towards him. He was wearing a long overcoat, holding his arms out by his sides.

'Who the hell are you?'

'You remember me, don't you? I came to talk to you at your house. I'm DI Frank Miller. Kim Smith's husband. I'm your other target. But Kim Smith is called Kim Miller now. She wasn't driving the car of course. That was one of my officers with a doll in the car seat.'

'Now I remember. If I don't get her, I still get paid for taking you down.'

'Venus Molloy has been taken into custody. She's your paymaster. You shoot me and you'll have done it for nothing.'

'I'm going to have to shoot you anyway, so I can get away.'

'Don't be silly, Larry. You're not going anywhere. Look around you.'

Two snipers were looking over the wall from up above where the railway tracks were. One sniper had come round from the side of a stone structure that housed electrical transformers. The back doors of a van opened, and a sniper was on one knee.

'They're all pointing at you, Larry, and even if they all take a shot, they won't hit me or each other. Just you.'

Larry was still standing holding the gun at his side.

'Those guys will take you out before you even have a chance to think about shooting me.'

Larry let his shoulders slump. 'I miss Constance. Scramble killed her. We were going to be together again. Now we can be together forever.'

He put the gun in his mouth and pulled the trigger.

FORTY-SIX

CHRISTMAS DAY

'I know that I will never be able to make up to you the hard feelings I caused, but I hope you enjoy this, and I want you to know I love you more than anything. And I'm sorry I doubted you. Merry Christmas.'

Kim handed him the box.

'Thank you. I just want you to know something.'

'What?'

'I didn't get you anything.'

She laughed and slapped him on the arm. He gave her a box, a little smaller than the one she'd given him. She opened it and smiled at the glittering diamond earrings. 'Thank you. They're beautiful.'

He opened his box. It was a TAG Heuer Carrera, with a blue face.

'I don't know what to say. This is fantastic.'

'I wanted to push the boat out. I should have trusted you, but I let my jealousy get in the way. I'm sorry, Frank.'

'Hey, it's fine. You didn't have to get me a nice watch to say sorry.'

'Oh, alright. I'll take it back.'

'Too late,' he said, taking it out of the box.

'Oh, and don't be doing anything stupid like that again. You and my father coming up with that plan to get Larry Cresswell.'

'Give kudos to your father; he made one phone call and his undercover team sprang into action. A few barriers, a temporary traffic light and a couple of vans.'

'Not to mention blocking off the streets after he'd passed by in his plumber's van.'

'Ian Powers found out that Venus was a fake, a lot easier than I did.'

'I'm glad it's over now.'

'And I wasn't even there! Thank God, Steffi Walker is fearless!'

'She's being promoted to detective sergeant as of January first. She deserves it.'

'She does that. Is she going to the party tonight?'

'Yes. And Julie Stott. Percy is looking forward to having us all round. Even Jeni's coming.'

Kim came over and sat on his lap. 'I love you, Frank Miller.'

'I love you too. And I love our daughters. And don't you ever worry; I'm not going anywhere.'

'Let's go and get them. Emma will be glad to know Santa's been.' She got up and went through to the bedroom to get the children.

Miller looked up at the dresser where the photograph of Carol was displayed.

'Merry Christmas,' he said to her.

AFTERWORD

Well, here we are at the end of another Miller. I hope you enjoyed this novel. The title was taken from the title of a Coldplay track on their album, A Rush of Blood to the Head.

I would like to thank the usual gang for their support and in no particular order they are, Tracey Devonshire, Julie Stott, Wendy Haines, Louise Unsworth Murphy, Jeni Bridge, Evelyn Bell, Merrill Astill Blount, Vanessa Kerrs, Michelle Barragan and last but not least, Fiona and Adrian Jackson.

Thank you to my wife and daughters who are always there for me and put up with me talking to myself and constantly running ideas by them.

AFTERWORD

I would also like to give a big shout out to each and every one of my readers. You are all fantastic. Many thanks to all of you who have given me a review for my books. If I could please ask you to leave an honest review for this book, that would be fantastic. Reviews are important for an indie author like me, and every one is appreciated.

All the best my friends.

John Carson
New York
July 2018

ABOUT THE AUTHOR

John Carson is originally from Edinburgh, Scotland, but now lives in New York State with his wife and family. And two dogs. And four cats.

website - johncarsonauthor.com
  Facebook - JohnCarsonAuthor
  Twitter - JohnCarsonBooks
  Instagram - JohnCarsonAuthor

Printed in Great Britain
by Amazon